HIDDEN AGENDAS

Proof Reading and Editing
Elizabeth A. Anken

Printed in the United States of America by
Booksurge Publishing

ISBN: 978-0-615-23920-0

Dedication

This book is dedicated to my wife Karen, my late father Plinio (Charlie), and mother Pearl. To my wife for providing the support and encouragement to complete this book. To my parents for the times we shared together and the life long memories. To them, my thanks for giving me a sense of humor and the motivation to pursue my dreams. And this book cannot be complete without acknowledging my Heavenly Father, from whom all Blessings are given.

Table of Contents

1

John Hurley, an ambitious lawyer fresh out of mid-west law school, had his eye on a job prospect with a big name NYC law firm. John's offered the job of a lifetime, but Norm Lasher, a stranger from John's past, turns up with plans of his own for John.

John doesn't realize the big problem on his hands when he agrees to meet Lasher in a bar to get *re-acquainted*. The problem gets worse when John is arrested the following morning and booked for Lasher's murder.

With his career and life on the line, John hires Jack Dausman, a big time attorney with connections to represent him. The principal partner of the NYC firm finds himself subpoenaed to appear at John's trial. Ironically, he finds himself on the opposite side of the courtroom being accused in Lasher's murder.

Chapter 1: New York, New York

The sound of the alarm clock interrupted the quietness of the morning before the sun had a chance to filter into the room from the voids between the hotel curtains and the adjacent walls. John Hurley grabbed an early shower, dressed for success, and took the elevator from his hotel room to the lobby below. An ambitious lawyer fresh out of a mid-west law school, John was ready to experience a high profile and glamorous life style in criminal law and the fast pace of big city life. Except for the early morning taxies and building maintenance workers cleaning up from the previous night's activities, the streets were nearly deserted. Rather than hailing a cab, he decided to walk the eight blocks to uptown Manhattan for his job interview. He grabbed a bagel, a fresh cup of coffee, and directions from a nearby convenience store before heading uptown.

The walk and fresh air is what he needed to settle his nerves and offer him solitude to ascertain the barrage of questions that were soon to be thrown at him. And just as important, the early start gave John ample time to enjoy the sights and sounds and for the city to make its impression on him.

John stared up at the towering walls of glass and steel enveloped in early morning haze as he reached his destination at 54th and Lexington Avenue. The sunlight filtered through the lobby leaving a random pattern of light and shadows on the floor as he entered the building.

"Good morning, may I help you?" came the groggy voice of a man getting up from behind the security desk.

"Yes, I have an appointment with Latchford, Bergman and Associates," John replied.

"They're on the 50th floor. Sign in here first and then take one of the elevators up to their offices," stated the security guard, pushing the sign-in log towards John and lazily pointing in the direction of the elevators, before sitting back down.

The high speed elevator ride to the 50th floor brought John directly into the lobby of the law office. "May I help you Sir?" was the greeting from a young woman with a sensuous voice and smile from behind the reception desk.

"Yes, I have a 9:00 appointment with Mr. Christopher Daniels," replied John, gazing at her to see if she was as attractive looking as her voice implied, returning the smile.

"Please be seated and I will let him know that you have arrived," she said.

John couldn't sit down. "Wow. Is she hot!" he thought to himself, walking around the lobby several times to view the office interior and wall of photographs of Who's Who in the firm.

"Sir, please follow me," motioned the receptionist, making her way from behind the desk and past John.

"You will be meeting in the conference room. Mr. Daniels is on a conference call and will be joining you in about 10 minutes. Meanwhile, have a seat. I need you to fill out this employment application. You know, the usual questions," she said, leaning over and placing the forms on the conference room table next to John.

"Can I get you a cup of coffee, juice, or water?" she inquired, looking at John.

"No thank you. I'm fine for now," returned John, as he absorbed the lingering aroma from her perfume.

"Well, if you need anything, just let me know," she continued, turning and heading back to the lobby.

A rush of anxiety overcame him as he walked over to the wall of glass and gazed out at the white mist encircling the room, limiting his view of the adjacent buildings and to the street below, fifty stories up.

"Hello John, I'm Christopher Daniels," said Daniels, as he put his hand on John's shoulder.

"Oh!" replied John as he turned around, somewhat startled. "I didn't hear you. I guess I was so caught up with the view from here."

"Yes, it is quite spectacular, even surrounded in haze. But fortunately it burns off quickly. Anyway, welcome to New York City," responded Daniels, looking John straight in the eyes and giving him a firm hand shake.

"Pull up a chair. We'll get started as soon as a few junior partners join us," he continued.

Daniels was a slender man in his late forties with the typical Hollywood movie look. His face was smooth with a dark, even tan underlying a two-day beard growth. A Bluetooth earpiece was slightly protruding from his ear, partially hidden by his finger-combed, shoulder-length brown hair, which was kept in place with a light touch of styling gel.

Before the door could shut and John could pull up a chair and sit down, he was bombarded with the usual warm up questions from three other people scrambling into the room with coffee cups and notepads in hand.

"Hello, I'm Bill Davis."

"I'm Robin Johnson."

"Hi John, Ted Caughlin."

After introducing themselves and shaking John's hand, they each made their way around the conference table and sat down.

"When did you get in?" asked Robin, opening her laptop and plugging in her wireless internet connection.

"Last night about 9:30," replied John.

"Is this your first trip to New York?" asked Ted.

"Yes," responded John to the continued series of questions.

"Can I get you something to drink?" asked Bill.

"Water would be fine, thank you," replied John.

Daniels pulled up a chair directly across from John and took out a copy of John's resume. "Before we get started, let me give you a brief history of the firm and the types of litigation we specialize in," stated Daniels. After what seemed to be twenty minutes of a one-sided conversation, Daniels concluded, "That's pretty much it in a nutshell, so let's move on, unless there are any questions."

"No," responded John, reaching for the bottled water on the table.

"Let me be blunt if I may," Daniels said. "We're a high profile firm with a very discrete list of clientele, ranging from top politicians to the hottest Hollywood celebrities and pop stars in the entertainment business. If we decide to bring someone new into the firm, it's through a referral from a respected board member or, as an example, the Dean of Harvard Law School. But once in a while, a resume comes across my desk that I feel deserves a response."

"We received a copy of your resume along with a referral letter, a copy of your college transcripts, and LSAT scores. The consensus is we were impressed with what we saw and decided to have you come in for an interview and meet," continued Daniels.

"Why do you want to work with a large firm like Latchford and Bergman? Certainly there are plenty of opportunities to work in a smaller firm back home where you can gain experience and have more opportunities for advancement," inquired Ted.

"And less stressful, if I might add," interjected Bill.

"Yes there are, but I grew up in the mid-west and I'm tired of it. I'm interested in relocating to a large metro area like New York City, someplace where I can be challenged," John responded.

"Do you have a girlfriend back home?" interjected Robin.

"No. Not right now," responded John.

"That's good. She'd break up with you after two weeks anyway. There's no such thing as a long term relationship when you're starting out. Especially in NYC and with this firm," Robin continued.

"Oh come on!" interjected Ted. "I don't recall you dumping your boyfriend after you started with the firm," he continued, with a smug grin and then a short self-indulgent laugh.

"Ted, I said long term relationships, not short term. You are such a jerk," Robin blurted out, shaking her head and giving Ted a dirty look.

Bill Davis quickly changed the direction the conversation was heading and proceeded to get it back on track.

"Don't let the glamour of the big city lure you into a life you're not ready to handle. I believe what Robin was getting at was commitment. There's a high price to pay working for a firm this size. It will crave every hour of your personal life, day and night, weekdays and weekends, and then demand more when you have nothing left to give. And as for the cost of living, your starting salary will barely cover your living expenses."

The back and forth barrage of questions and answers continued. The meeting was shorter than John had anticipated, or maybe it only seemed to be. It ended abruptly when Daniels got a call on his Bluetooth and had to cut the meeting short.

"Thanks for coming in. We'll be in touch," stated Daniels, briskly shaking John's hand as he folded up his notebook and headed onto other pressing matters.

"Hey, gotta run too," replied Ted, reaching across the table and shaking John's hand.

"Me too," replied Robin, removing the wireless internet connection and powering off her notebook. "Mr. Daniels doesn't like to drag things out. Either way, you won't have to wait long for a response."

"Nice meeting you. Good luck," Bill blurted out, as he hurriedly followed behind Robin.

Chapter 2: Expectations

The 3-hour flight home, coupled with the refills of cocktails, gave John time to reflect on the interview. It didn't seem long enough for John to make the impression on them he had planned. What could he have said or done differently? As the number of drinks increased, so did his feeling of frustration with himself. Then something he never thought of asking during the interview hit him – how did Daniels get his resume and who recommended him for a position with the firm? It never dawned on John to ask.

During the flight he attempted to discuss his interview with the stewardess several times, perhaps subconsciously looking for feedback. "Sorry you didn't get the job," responded the stewardess in a sympathetic voice, as John descended from the plane. "Good luck."

The first week home passed slowly, and then the second week. Persistent walks to the mail box in anticipation of a job offer soon faded and life was back to normal, or as normal as could be expected. Hit squarely in the face with reality, John tried to put the experience aside and sat down to look for a less glamorous job closer to home. Picking up several employment letters he had written the previous week, John headed out the door.

"Hey John, wait up," yelled a voice. John looked up to see the mailman, two doors down, walking briskly towards him waving his arms.

"Hey John, you got a registered letter. I think it's the one you've been looking for," said the mailman, gasping to catch his breath. John's eyes gleamed with excitement as he grabbed for the letters and shuffled through them until he found it. "Thanks," he replied, "Thanks."

John peered at the envelope. "It's from Latchford and Bergman," he said out loud before pushing his finger under the flap and tearing it open. He hesitantly pulled the letter out. His eyes hurriedly scanned each word until he found what he was looking for, or not looking for - When can you start? John's eyes grew wide as he read it again, this time slower, not believing what he had read.

"This can't be? These things just don't happen," John said to himself. "Yes! Yes!" he yelled, flinging his left arm into the air with a closed fist.

Chapter 3: Old Friends Reunited

Packing was the easy part. A new career and life meant leaving the old behind for the taking. Of course, there wasn't much to take or leave behind. As the boxes of odds and ends to be discarded filled, the telephone rang. John caught it on the eighth ring. Waiting to grab his breath he answered. "Hello, John Hurley."

"Hey, John, I hear you've been offered a job with one of the most prestigious, high profile law firms in the Big Apple. Congratulations," was the response of a man's voice on the other end.

"Who am I talking to?" replied John.

"Well, I don't know if you'd remember me, but we share a common interest. We're like old lost friends," came a voice on the other end, in a somewhat mixed laugh and sarcastic tone. "The name's Lasher, Norman Lasher. I have a proposition for you."

"What?" replied John.

"Meet me, let's say, 9:30 at Mahley's Bar. You know where that is John? I'll be in the back playing pool and having a few drinks."

The telephone went silent, followed by the sound of the dial tone. John sluffed off the call as a prank and tried not to pay attention to it. As the evening passed,

8:30, 8:45, 9:00… John grabbed his hat and flew out the door heading to the bar. "Who the heck is Norman Lasher?" he asked himself.

Arriving at the bar, John located the pool room through the haze of smoke and empty tables at the rear of the building and walked back.

"John, over here," came a gravely voice from behind the pool table in the far corner.

Through the haze of smoke and dim lighting John made out the figure of a staunchly older gentleman leaning over the table smoking a cigarette. "Do you play pool John? It helps reduce tension," Lasher said.

"No. Do I know you?" responded John.

"Fill this up," said Lasher, handing John an empty glass that was resting against the edge of the table. "Make it a scotch. Get yourself something too and have the bartender put it on my tab. It's time we got reacquainted."

John got Lasher a refill and put it on the table. "Pull up a chair and tell me about your new career with this New York City law firm. You must be excited?" replied Lasher.

Taken back, John glared at Lasher as he leaned forward to get up. "How do you know that?" responded John.

"It doesn't matter how I found out," replied Lasher.

"Look Lasher, or whatever your name is, I don't know what your game is, but..."

"Early retirement, John," replied Lasher, clutching John by the arm and pushing him back into his chair. "Now sit down, shut up, and listen."

"You don't remember me, do you? I know it has been a while, and I've gotten fatter, I drink more, and my hair, well, let's not talk about my hair," he said, rubbing his hand over the balding top of his head.

"Think back to your law school, or should I be more precise John, the day you sat for your LSAT exam," stated Lasher, stroking his fingers up and down the pool cue.

"Come on John, think back. It wasn't that long ago. You don't recall what happened on that day? The phony bomb threat that forced the evacuation of the entire building. That was certainly an unfortunate situation, but look at the bright side. The exam had to be cancelled and rescheduled," continued Lasher.

"Well John, is your memory coming back? Take a closer look at me. I'm the guy who collected all the uncompleted exam booklets that afternoon, all 83 of them. Only thing was, I only collected 82 - one was missing. Oh, I admit, it took me some time to put the pieces together and narrow down who took it, but I will leave the particulars up to you," he went on, pausing several times to take a drink.

"I've been watching you for some time, and frankly, you're not as bright as I initially perceived you to be.

The only way you could have passed the exam was by cheating," said Lasher.

"You're mistaken," John blurted out. "I don't know what the hell you're talking about and I don't have to sit here and listen to your accusations."

"Yeah, I could have turned you in...," continued Lasher.

"Well, why didn't you?" replied John.

"Money John, money. I've been sitting on this for just the right time. Now my nest egg is about to hatch," replied Lasher

"Read between the lines John. I know how to keep my mouth shut, for a price that is. It would be an unfortunate turn of events if your new employers heard that your impressive grades and career development were not achieved, in let's just say, under the most honest circumstances. Where I come from, it's called cheating. Even if it couldn't be proven, your career of a lifetime with this big time firm would be questionable, wouldn't it?" prodded Lasher.

"Shut up, just shut the hell up," John blurted out, pushing his chair back against the wall and standing up.

"Think about it, but don't wait too long. I took the liberty of jotting my home number on the back of the napkin," replied Lasher in a smug tone of voice, as he put it on the table and passed it to John.

John pushed back his anger and stormed out of the bar. Lasher slouched back in his chair, clutching the pool cue, as he finished his cigarette and drink. Pulling a handkerchief from his pants pocket, he wrapped John's glass and put it in his coat. "Insurance," he mumbled to himself under his breath. "Insurance."

Chapter 4: The Morning After

Packed and ready to leave with suitcases in hand, John shut the door to his old life behind. Putting his suitcases in his car, he turned to notice two men walking up the driveway.

"Going somewhere?" asked one of the men.

"Sorry guys, whatever it is you want, you'll have to wait. I'm rushed for time to make a 3:30 flight to New York," John said, shutting the car trunk.

"You John Hurley?"

"Yes, who are..."

"Police. I'm detective LiCausi and this is officer Bauder."

"What's this about?" asked John.

"Just want to ask you a few questions. Do you know a guy named Norman Lasher?" inquired detective LiCausi.

"No, I've never heard of him. Should I?" replied John.

"You tell us," stated LiCausi.

"You say you don't know him. Funny, he knew you. He had a piece of paper in his coat pocket with your name and telephone number on it," Bauder said.

"You sure you didn't know this guy?" asked LiCausi again.

"Like I said, I've never heard of him," responded John. "I'm sure he's got me mixed up with someone else."

"Where were you last night?" questioned Bauder.

"Home, why? What are you getting at?" replied John.

"You say you didn't know this guy, yet he has your name and telephone number in his coat pocket."

"Then let's ask this guy Lasher, or whatever his name is," inquired Hurley.

"I don't think so. The guy's lying on a slab in the city morgue," said Bauder.

"He was stabbed to death last night around 11:30. And right now, you're our only suspect," stated LiCausi.

"By the way, we dusted the place for prints. For someone you say you've never met, do you want to tell us how one of the glasses found in his living room had your fingerprints all over it?" inquired LiCausi.

"You might want to call your travel agent and cancel your travel plans. You're not going to be needing those tickets," said Bauder.

"Turn around and put your hands above your head," ordered LiCausi. "You're under arrest for suspicion of murder. You'd better get yourself a good attorney."

Hurley was processed uptown - fingerprinted, photographed and booked on suspicion of murder. After calling his travel agent, John telephoned a local attorney, Jack Dausman.

"I'll get down there as soon as I can John," replied Dausman. "In the meantime, just sit tight and don't volunteer any information or answer any questions."

The rush-hour traffic was light, but it still took Dausman over two hours to get to the station.

"What kept you?" blurted out Hurley.

"Trying to get bail but..."

"So let's get out of here!" interrupted John, as he started for the door.

"Not so fast. I hit a dead end," said Dausman. "This guy Lasher you supposedly killed was well connected - a lot of influential friends in legal and political circles. I just got off the phone with the DA. He's convinced he has a solid case - all he needs to get a conviction for murder. And where I stand, it's pretty convincing. Sorry kid, but it looks like you'll be here for awhile, at least until you can make bail or a Grand Jury date is set," said Dausman, motioning to the police officer that he was finished.

"That's the best I can do tonight. Try to get some sleep and I'll see you in the morning," Dausman continued, closing the cell door behind him, and leaving John to himself.

"Get some sleep. Yeah, right!" responded John.

The following morning Dausman arranged bail. With a Grand Jury date set, Dausman and John went over the evidence to corroborate their defense. "I'll do the best I can to defend you, but we're up against some overwhelming evidence. You need to be straight with me. Did you kill the guy?" asked Dausman.

"Absolutely not," responded John.

"Did you know him?" asked Dausman.

"No!...Well, I mean yes. No!" replied John.

"Well, what is it?" questioned Dausman.

"I never heard of the guy until he called. He wanted to meet to talk," said John.

"Talk about what?" interrupted Dausman.

"He said he had something on me that would ruin my career," said John.

"Did he?" inquired Dausman.

"No. I told you, I've never seen the guy before the other night," insisted John.

Dausman kept up the pressure. "They're going to call the bartender as a witness. When they get her on the stand she's going to say that you and Lasher argued and you threatened to kill him. What did you argue about?" asked Dausman.

"Money," said John.

"You mean blackmail, don't you?" interjected Dausman again. "Is that when you followed Lasher home?"

"No! I didn't follow him home. I've never been to his place," stated John.

"It isn't going to go favorably for you if you keep insisting that you've never been to Lasher's place. Either change your story or come up with how a glass with your fingerprints all over it ended up at the murder scene," demanded Dausman.

"How the hell should I know?" responded John, somewhat agitated. "Maybe he took my glass from the bar home with him."

"I somehow don't think so," Dausman stated with skepticism. "I was at Lasher's place this morning taking a look around. The glass with your finger prints on it is part of a series of five he has on display in his cabinet, not one of the cheap rummage sale glasses from Mahley's Bar."

Chapter 5: An Unsuspected Witness

The Grand Jury convened to review the evidence and to determine if the case should go to trial. Dausman got to the courthouse early to get comfortable. As John was brought in, he turned and glanced around the room as it filled with onlookers and reporters. John froze as his eyes panned towards the back of the room.

"It can't be?" John muttered to himself. "It just can't be." There was Christopher Daniels, his back slightly turned to John, as he was preparing to sit down.

"What's he doing here?" John asked himself in a trembling voice. John hurriedly made his way over to Dausman and sat down. He nervously slouched in his chair trying not to be noticed. But it was too late. As Daniels turned to sit down, he glanced up towards the front of the courtroom and made eye contact with John.

"Sit up straight," said Dausman, as he patted John on the back. "And get comfortable. We're going to be here a while."

The DA presented the opening statement to the jury, outlining the evidence against Hurley. He informed them it was their duty to judge the case on the evidence provided, and if they find reasonable evidence Hurley committed the murder, he would be bound over for trial. Having little in the way of defense or rebuttal at that time, Dausman waived his opening statement.

The DA called his first witness - Mary Ann Pirano, the bartender at Mahley's Bar. After establishing Pirano's identity and general background information for the jury, the DA began the interrogation.

"Did you know Norman Lasher?" questioned the DA.

"Yes," responded Pirano. "Norm was a frequent patron at Mahley's Bar, and he was such a nice man. He was soft spoken and very generous. Everyone liked Norm. He usually came in a couple of nights a week to have a few drinks and shoot pool. He said it relaxed him."

"What time did he come in on the night he was murdered?" asked the DA.

"His usual time, around 8:30 in the evening," responded Pirano.

"Was he alone?" asked the DA.

"Yes. Like I said, he bought a drink and went in the back to shoot pool. Then that guy over there came in," said Pirano, pointing at John Hurley.

"Let the record show that the witness is pointing to the defendant John Hurley," stated the DA.

"Then what happened?" asked the DA.

"They had a drink and sat in the back talking," said Pirano.

"Do you know that they talked about?" interjected the DA.

"No, but it must have been something. They started arguing and then all of a sudden the defendant started throwing chairs around and screaming. He told Norm that if he didn't keep his mouth shut he would kill him. He was yelling so loudly everyone in the bar heard him," stated Pirano.

"That's not true! She's lying," John blurted out in a raised voice, pushing his chair back, standing up, and looking at Pirano with a cold stare.

"Mr. Hurley, sit down. Any further outbursts and I will have you removed from the courtroom," ordered the Judge, pounding his gavel on the bench.

"Sorry your Honor. It won't happen again," assured Dausman, grabbing John's arm and directing him to sit down.

"What did Lasher do?" asked the DA.

"Norm finished his drink and left shortly after the defendant. He seemed agitated and in a hurry to get home," responded Pirano.

"Anything else?" continued the DA.

"Yeah," said Pirano. "The defendant over there came back about 15 minutes later looking for Norm. He asked me where he lived, but I kept my mouth shut. I didn't want to get involved. I could tell he was looking to make trouble."

"You're a liar!" exclaimed John, as he started to get up from his seat, but was restrained by Dausman.

"I'm not going to warn you again. One more outburst and I will have the marshal remove you. Do I make myself clear?" threatened the Judge in a raised voice, repeatedly pounding his gavel on the bench.

"Yes your Honor," stated John, as he sat back down.

"No further questions of this witness." stated the DA.

"Do you wish to cross examine?" asked the Judge, gazing at Dausman. "Not at this time," Dausman responded.

"I call my next witness, Mr. Christopher Daniels," stated the DA. After the general formalities, he began questioning Daniels.

"Yes, I knew Norman Lasher," replied Daniels. "He was a respected friend and colleague, and well liked within the legal and political circles. But I don't understand why I was subpoenaed to be here."

"I'll get to that shortly," said the DA. "How did you meet Lasher?"

"We met when I was studying law. Norman worked at the University. You could say that he was my mentor. He was a brilliant man," responded Daniels.

"Do you know the defendant, John Hurley?" asked the DA.

"Yes." responded Daniels. "He interviewed for a position with the New York City law firm I am a partner with, about two weeks ago."

"How did you hear about the defendant? Did he submit his resume for a job interview?" asked the DA again.

"No, I contacted John and set up an interview as a favor to Norman Lasher," replied Daniels.

"Interesting," replied the DA. "In an affidavit the defendant made to the detectives earlier, he swore he never knew Lasher until they met in Mahley's Bar. Yet, it was Lasher that landed him an interview with your law firm. Why would someone you've never met do that, unless you knew each other," stated the DA, in a forceful and outspoken tone of voice. "By the way, did your firm hire him?"

"We recently made him an offer to join the firm, but with everything that has happened, I don't know if he had time to consider it," responded Daniels.

"No further questions, your witness," stated the DA, staring in Dausman's direction as he walked to his chair.

Chapter 6: The Motive

Dausman recalled Pirano to the stand for cross examination.

"Much of the evidence heard so far has been circumstantial," stated Dausman, strolling slowly past the jury box, looking directly at the jurors. "The crux of the case against my client rests on one piece of evidence only - the glass found in Lasher's house." Dausman turned and looking at Pirano, approached the witness stand.

"In an earlier statement you said that the defendant and Lasher had a drink in the back and talked. Did Lasher drink alone or did the defendant also have a drink?" questioned Dausman.

"They both had a drink," responded Pirano.

"How many?" interrupted Dausman.

"I believe they each had one," stated Pirano.

"Who cleaned up the area after the defendant and Lasher left?" continued Dausman.

"I did," responded Pirano.

"I want you to think carefully about the next question. How many glasses were on the table when you cleaned it off?" asked Dausman.

Pirano rotated her neck a couple of times to relax and fidgeted as she thought about the question. "Well, two, of course," replied Pirano.

"Are you sure there were two glasses and not just one glass?" inquired Dausman.

"No. There were two glasses. I remember picking them up," Pirano stated with confidence.

"Do you remember anything different about the glasses?" inquired Dausman.

"What do you mean?" questioned Pirano.

"Were they typical bar glasses or was there anything different about one of the glasses?" continued Dausman.

"Typcial bar glasses," replied Pirano.

"I stopped by Mahley's Bar the other night. In fact, the same day of the week the defendant and Lasher met.

It was a busy place. You were rushing from one end of the bar to the other trying to keep up with the orders. With all the commotion, I was surprised you didn't have someone helping you."

"Oh, after eight years as a bartender, I'm used to it. Anyone else behind the bar would only get in my way," stated Pirano.

"But with all the commotion, isn't it possible for someone to bring in their own glass and not notice the difference?" continued Dausman.

"I object. The defendant's attorney is leading the witness," interjected the DA.

"Over-ruled. I'll let the witness answer the question," ordered the Judge.

"Yes, I suppose, but the night Norm and the defendant argued, it was an off night and the bar was mostly empty," stated Pirano.

Dausman started to walk to his chair, but stopped short and turned back to look at Pirano. "In an earlier statement you made to the DA, you said that you heard the defendant arguing with Norman Lasher in the back of the bar and that you heard him threaten to kill Lasher. Is that correct," questioned Dausman.

"Yes, I believe so, if that is what I said," answered Pirano.

"The pool room where the defendant and Lasher were arguing is located in the back of the bar, a considerable distance from where your were working.

I talked to several people that were in the back playing pool the night the defendant and Lasher were arguing. They said they remember the defendant and Lasher arguing, but they never heard the defendant threaten Lasher. What they recall was the defendant telling Lasher that if he didn't stay away from him, he would go to the police and file a complaint," continued Dausman.

"I object. The information is purely hearsay and inadmissible," interrupted the DA.

"The witnesses are present in the courtroom, and if necessary, I can call them to testify," stated Dausman, directing his response to the DA.

"Over-ruled," ordered the Judge, motioning Dausman to continue.

"I am asking you to think about your earlier statement. Are you sure you heard the defendant threaten to kill Lasher," questioned Dausman.

"Well, I heard them arguing, but I'm not sure if I actually heard the defendant threatened Norm," responded Pirano.

"Dausman started to dismiss the witness, but paused. In a curious tone of voice, he said "Only one more question. Before today, do you recognize anyone else here in the courtroom?"

"Well, I've seen that guy in the back that was being questioned by the DA earlier," stated Pirano, pointing to Christopher Daniels.

"Let the record show that the witness is referring to Mr. Christopher Daniels," directed Dausman.

"When was that?" continued Dausman, looking directly at Pirano.

"I think it was on the day that Norm was killed. Yeah, except around 11:00 in the morning. I saw him and Norm leaving a restaurant down the block when I was just getting to work," replied Pirano.

"Do you know what they were doing?" inquired Dausman.

"No, like I said, I was just getting to work and they were leaving," repeated Pirano.

"I have no further questions," stated Dausman. "I recall Christopher Daniels to the stand."

Daniels took the stand again.

"Well, what a revelation. When you were on the witness stand earlier, you never mentioned that you and Lasher had met on the morning of his murder. I'm curious, what was so important that you had to come all the way out here from New York City that you couldn't discuss over the phone?"

"Like I stated earlier, Norman and I were good friends. I had some vacation time and I owed him a visit. I didn't see any relevance in mentioning it," responded Daniels.

"Let me play a long shot and see if I can explain why you came all the way out here from New York City to meet with Lasher and who murdered him," said Dausman.

"Stop me if you think I've left anything out, but I believe you killed Lasher, not the defendant," stated Dausman, looking Daniels straight in the eye.

"That's absurd," stated Daniels, laughing.

"Lasher was blackmailing you, wasn't he?" continued Dausman.

"I don't know what you're talking about," replied Daniels in a smug and elusive tone.

"Let me continue. Lasher called you to pressure you to interview the defendant for a position with your law firm. You suspected that he was out to blackmail the defendant just like he was blackmailing you. You didn't have any success in dealing with Lasher over the phone, so you decided meet with him and try to cut a deal," stated Dausman.

"That's ridiculous. Norman and I were good friends," interjected Daniels.

"No you weren't," stated Dausman. "You hated Lasher and you were tired of having him drain you financially. You only agreed to hire the defendant if he would stop harassing and blackmailing you."

"That's not true," repeated Daniels, in a cool and collective tone. "Not a bit of what you're saying is true. You don't have any evidence to substantiate these accusations."

"I'm getting to the evidence," responded Dauseman.

"You reluctantly hired the defendant, John Hurley, but Lasher reneged on his promise to quit blackmailing you. That angered you and you had enough of him leaching off of you. So you flew out here to meet with Lasher to pressure him to end it. You met with him, but you weren't able to persuade Lasher to quit, were you?" questioned Dausman.

"Lasher didn't want to have anything to do with you, and that really angered you. The bartender earlier testified that she saw you and Lasher together the day Lasher was killed." stated Dausman.

"So Norman and I got together earlier in the day. I owed Norman a visit," interrupted Daniels again. But Dausman persisted.

"You knew that later that same evening Lasher had an appointment to meet with Hurley because Lasher bragged about what he was up to. You saw this as your one opportunity to kill Lasher and put an end to his harassment. You had the motive and the guy to take the fall. You decided to wait for him and surprise him when he returned home after meeting with the defendant. That's when you murdered him!" exclaimed Dausman.

"Again, not a word of what you are saying is true," responded Daniels, in an argumentative tone of voice. "The defendant's fingerprints were found on a glass at Norman's place. Hurley murdered him."

The glass!" said Dausman. "I'm glad you brought that up. It's the only solid piece of evidence that the DA has used to build his case against the defendant. The bartender stated that Lasher had several drinks while he was shooting pool prior to meeting with the defendant. She also stated that Lasher and the defendant each had only one drink together at the bar. The police report indicated that they only found one glass on the table next to Lasher's body and that the defendants fingerprints were the only set of prints on it. Doesn't that seem odd that Lasher didn't have a drink and that his fingerprints weren't on the glass along with the defendants?" inquired Dausman.

"So what does that prove? That doesn't mean I killed Lasher. As you just stated, that was Hurley's glass," argued Daniels.

"You're right, said Dausman. "Let's just speculate for a moment. Suppose Lasher switched the bar glass with one he brought from home. He bought the defendant a drink and had the bartender refill his glass. Lasher picked up the defendant's glass after the argument, being ever so careful not to smudge the fingerprints and took it with him, leaving the two original bar glasses behind. That would account for the glass found later at Lasher's place with the defendant's fingerprints on it," said Dausman.

As Dausman started to walk back to his seat, he turned and looked at Daniels. "Oh, I forgot to mention the interesting part. In reviewing the police report, it noted that their lab analysis found traces of linen on the glass. They matched it to the same linen from Lasher's handkerchief found in his coat pocket."

"Now for the motive," said Dausman, approaching the witness box, looking straight at Daniels. "What did

Lasher have on you that put you in a position to be blackmailed? It wasn't until you mentioned that you knew Lasher from your law school that things started to come together. The defendant told me earlier why Lasher wanted to meet with him at Mahley's bar. Lasher was attempting to blackmail him the same way he was blackmailing you. He believed that John Hurley had cheated on his LSAT exam to get into law school and threatened to ruin his career if he didn't agree to pay him to keep his mouth shut. Lasher was a predator and knew how to extort money from people."

Dausman turned, made brief eye contact with each of the jurors, and then continued. "There is no shred of proof that the defendant ever cheated on the LSAT or any other exam. In fact, John Hurley had taken the LSAT a total of three times before he scored a high enough grade to be admitted to law school. He had to work hard and struggled to make it through law school. But he did so without cheating on anything," continued Dausman.

"What does that have to do with me. So I knew Norman. Like I said, we knew each other from law school," inserted Daniels.

"I'm glad you brought that up again," stated Dausman. "We contacted the Law Department at the University, and with their assistance and a subpoena, we were able to obtain a copy of your LSAT scores and college grades. I have them right there," stated Dausman, pointing to the folders on the table. "I reviewed your LSAT scores and I was surprised to find them marginal, to say the least. You barely passed, but your college grades were impressive. Tell me, how can someone who barely passed the LSAT exam be on the honor roll as many times as you were?"

"I applied myself," replied Daniels.

"I don't think so," responded Dausman, in a raised tone of voice. "As you mentioned, Lasher worked at the University. In fact, he worked in the law school office. You and he became such good friends that he provided you with copies of the class exam questions prior to the tests. And working in the law school as long as he had, he was able to, as you stated earlier, mentor you. That's how you managed to pass and graduate with honors, wasn't it? You didn't apply yourself, you cheated! And now that you are a successful lawyer, Lasher felt he owned you. That's when he started blackmailing you. Isn't that right?" hammered Dausman.

"You can't prove anything. It's still all speculation on your part," stated Daniels, pressing forward in the witness box in a confrontational tone.

Chapter 7: A Career Adjustment

"As a lawyer, you know that I don't have to prove that you killed Lasher. I just have to prove beyond reasonable doubt that the defendant John Hurley wasn't the only person with a motive and opportunity," stated Dausman, as he turned and approached the jury box.

Dausman walked past the jury box, pausing to look at each member of the jury as he prepared to make his closing statement.

"The defendant John Hurley isn't guilty of murder," Dausman stated to the jury. "And John Hurley certainly isn't guilty of cheating on his LSAT to be accepted to law school. The folders on the table contain statements from his university professors and classmates. Any one of them can be called as character witnesses to attest to the defendant's hard work and dedication to graduate with only one goal - to practice law. He isn't guilty of murder."

"We have a witness who testified seeing Daniels and Lasher leaving a restaurant together the day Lasher was murdered," said Dausman. "And if we need to, we can subpoena both Daniel's and Lasher's bank statements. I'm sure the DA and the police will find all they need to prove that Daniels was being blackmailed and sufficient motive to hold him for Lasher's murder. It is your responsibility to review all of the evidence presented, and if there is any reasonable doubt as to whether the defendant John Hurley murdered Norman Lasher, then you are obligated to release him, pending the outcome of further investigation."

It didn't take the jury long to reach a decision. They found insufficient evidence to hold Hurley for the murder of Lasher at this time. He was released pending further investigation of Daniels by the DA's office and the police.

"Well John," said Dausman, patting him on the back. "It has been a long day. Let's get out of here. Sorry things didn't work out for you the way you planned, but look at the positive side. You won't be facing murder charges. I'll let you know when we need to be back in court. Just don't make any plans to leave town until then."

Dausman packed his briefcase and proceeded to walk to the courtroom doors. As he started through, he stopped short, turned, and glanced back at John. "What do you think you will do now?"

"I'm not sure. I took some engineering courses in college," stated Hurley.

"Well, let's consider all the facts. You didn't cheat on your LSAT and you graduated in the top one-third of your class. I wouldn't recommend pursuing a career in engineering. But there is one you're well qualified for," stated Dausman.

"What's that, politics?" inquired John.

"Politics?" questioned Dausman, in a joking tone of voice.

"No John, the practice of Law. I believe you have the abilities to make an excellent attorney. That is, with the proper guidance. We start work at 8:30 a.m. sharp. I'll see you tomorrow morning in my office," replied Dausman, as the courtroom doors slowly closed behind him.

The End

The
Coin Collector

2

Charlie, now in his mid-eighties, has been living alone since his wife passed away twenty-seven years earlier. To supplement his retirement and cover his cost of living, he rents the upstairs of his house to college students and occasionally works at a local golf course.

His social life involves taking the bus to the mall to meet up with friends for coffee and pass the time; that is until he met Tanya. A seductive, drug-addicted prostitute, she has only one thing on her mind, latching onto older men like Charlie and milking them out of their life's savings.

With the aid of two street punks, Ray and Earl, she plans to steal Charlie's coin collection. With the coin collection in hand, the two punks soon realize it isn't exactly what they expected.

Chapter 1: The Ladies' Man

The early morning rays of sun bent around the window blind to gain access to the dark interior of the bedroom where Charlie was sleeping. The room was stale from the night heat and lack of air movement. The fan sat silent on the dresser with the cord unplugged from the wall outlet. Charlie woke and gazed at the clock sitting on the night stand next to the bed to find out the time. He laid in bed for several minutes deciding if he should get up or try to go back to sleep.

"Oh boy," he said in a low voice, still half asleep as he pushed the sheets off. Nature had made the decision for him. He sat up on the edge of the bed, massaged his balding head, and yawned. The cream-colored short sleeve cotton undershirt was stained from sweat and frayed, reflecting its age. Charlie maneuvered out of bed and rubbed his crotch as he headed to the bathroom to urinate.

After relieving himself, Charlie turned on the fluorescent light above the kitchen table to prepare breakfast. The momentary hesitation and flickering eventually gave the additional illumination to augment the natural light from the window at the sink. The kitchen was dated with worn out materials and outdated appliances, reminiscent of the rest of the house. The light from the two bulb fluorescent fixture bounced off the leaf green and beige cabinets and terrazzo patterned plastic laminate countertop. A round table Charlie had picked up from a bargain store was pushed into the corner of the kitchen next to the radiator. Three tubular metal chairs with plastic cushions were arranged around it.

Charlie selected two medium oranges from the basket on the counter, cut them in half, and pressed them into the plastic orange juice squeezer. From the refrigerator, he took out a container of mixed fruits and combined it with the fresh orange juice. That, along with a cup of coffee and a pecan tart or several cookies, made up his morning breakfast - enough to carry him over until late morning.

The two story house, termed by his friends as Fort Knox, was situated on a corner lot in Portsmouth, now incorporated into the City of Kingston. Charlie rented the upstairs three rooms to college students to supplement his retirement check and offset the cost of utilities and taxes. Now in his mid-eighties, Charlie lived alone since his wife Pearl had passed away 25 years earlier. Regardless of that, Charlie had a lot of energy and was very sociable. He was fond of flirting with the ladies whenever he was out.

By 11:00 Charlie had changed to take the 11:15 bus uptown to the mall to meet up with chums at Wal-Mart for coffee, read the newspaper, and engage in general chit chat. He preferred to take the bus and leave his 1965 Chrysler New Yorker parked in the garage.

Charlie was a sharp dresser for today's standards, even though his clothes were outdated. His heavy leather soled wingtip shoes and bell bottom plaid pants were contrasted by the relatively new short sleeve polo shirt. Charlie was particular about his shirts; there had to be three buttons, not four.

After checking the windows to be sure they were closed and locked, Charlie turned the inside knob on the front door to the lock position as he closed it behind him. His side pocket bulged from the key ring which had a minimum of one key for each door, trunk, and suitcase in the house. He pulled it out and inserted the key into the mortise lock above the door knob and locked it. Then he double checked the knob again and pushed on the door to be sure it was securely locked. Charlie had the schedule down pat; a short walk to the corner bus stop to catch the bus and a 15-minute ride to the mall.

"Good morning Charlie. Looks like another hot one again today. You're not golfing today in this heat, are you?" came the greeting from the bus driver as Charlie handed him the fare.

"Not today. I'm just going to the mall for a couple of hours and pick up some groceries," responded Charlie, clutching the support pull as he turned to take a quick glance around at the passengers. It was mostly a mix of college students and senior citizens on their way up-town or to the mall.

"Sit down here," said the young woman, as she scooted over to make room for Charlie. "You're headed to the mall?" she inquired, with a gracious smile.

"To have coffee with some friends," Charlie's replied.

"I don't know what we would do without air conditioning. It's going to be another unbearably hot and muggy day. You live close by?" she inquired, engaging Charlie in conversation.

"Just up the street," responded Charlie.

"Close to the bus route, hey. How convenient. You don't drive?" she continued.

"Oh yeah, but it's just as easy to take the bus to the mall and leave the car in the garage," responded Charlie.

"I'm Tanya," she said smiling.

"Charlie," was his response.

"You're a golfer, are you?" inquired Tanya.

"I golf, but it's too hot today. Do you play golf?" replied Charlie.

"No, it's not for me," she replied back. "So, what do you like to do besides golf?" she asked.

"Oh, mostly golf. I give lessons at one of the local courses. To pass time I do some metal detecting around the area," said Charlie.

"That sounds interesting. I've seen people doing it in the parks. Is that where you go?" she continued.

"You can't find anything in the parks. They've been worked over. You need to look in older places," responded Charlie.

"What kinds of things have you found? Have you ever found anything really valuable?" she continued.

"Oh, an assortment of jewelry and old coins, mostly mixed in with a lot of junk. But I have found a few valuable coins," replied Charlie.

"You keep them locked up in the bank, I hope?" questioned Tanya, prodding for a response, but not trying to appear pushy.

"No. I probably should, but they're hidden away in a safe place," said Charlie.

The brief stops to drop off and pick up passengers went by quickly as Tanya and Charlie continued in conversation.

"Have a good day. Maybe I'll see you again," said Tanya, smiling up at Charlie as the bus stopped at the mall entrance and Charlie prepared to get off.

"You too," returned Charlie.

Chapter 2: The Punks

The mall was an older style design and in decline, but well maintained. The no-name stores didn't attract the younger crowd. These features and the two anchors stores, Wal-Mart and Loblaws grocery, made it a convenient and comfortable place for senior citizens to get together.

Charlie headed through the entrance doors and down the corridor, passing by rows of seating dividing the corridor. Jack and John were quietly sitting outside of Wal-Mart, buried in sections of the local newspaper, waiting for Charlie.

"Ah, Charlie's here," blurted John in a low voice, peering up from the stock section in the newspaper to see Charlie making his way up the mall corridor.

"Time to get a cup and a bite to eat," Jack said, gathering the newspaper sections, as he and John got up.

"Morning," said Charlie, catching up with them.

"You're right on time," said John, looking at his watch.

The three made their way around the maze of merchandise displays blocking the center of Wal-Mart's aisles to the back of the store where the lunch area was located.

"Over here," said Jack in a high voice, waving in the direction where Bill was seated, and anxiously gazing around.

"I got us a table," Bill said, as he got up to join the three in the coffee line. Bill, John, and Jack each got a cup of black coffee and a muffin. Charlie ordered his usual - bacon, extra crispy, eggs over easy, and coffee - before sitting down with the group.

"Going golfing today Charlie?" asked Bill, emptying two containers of cream into his coffee.

"Too hot today," said Charlie, as he put a piece of bacon in his mouth. "Maybe later in the week."

"Disgusting, just disgusting," said Bill, holding up the front page of the morning paper. "It's the same depressing crap every day. Crime, drugs, murder, political corruption, continued violence in the Middle East. Where's it going? I don't know why I continue to spend money on it."

"What? You spend money? Who's kidding who? You probably found it sitting on the table when you got here," said Charlie jokingly.

"It's the same thing on TV. You can't turn the bloody thing on anymore without seeing the same thing over and over. The selection is horrible. Nothing but sex and violence," inserted Jack.

"Have you seen the stock section?" interrupted John, fumbling his way through the sections scattered on the floor beside Bill's chair.

"What are you looking for, to check on how much money you lost in the damn market again?" replied Jack.

"Ok guys, but if you want to make some serious money, you'd do what I did and invest in Google," responded John.

"What's Google?" asked Bill.

"It's an internet browser. You've heard of the internet, haven't you?" replied Jack.

"Talk about disgusting. Take a look at those two," stated Jack, motioning in the direction of two scruffy young men shuffling their way through the coffee line.

"Blue jeans two sizes too large and hanging below their waists, tattoos on their arms and necks, pierced eyebrows and faces, shaved heads, and headphones turned up so loud you can hear the rap crap they're listening to from here," he went on.

"It's certainly a different world than when we grew up. They're just looking for attention," remarked Charlie, as the group stared in their direction.

The group followed the two punks with their eyes, occasionally looking up to check on their progress as they proceeded through the line.

"They're loud punks. You name the drug, they're probably on it. If they sit around us, I'm leaving," said Bill, as he concentrated on finishing off his donut by dunking it in his cup of coffee.

"If you don't give them any attention, they won't bother you," returned Charlie.

The two men made their way between the tables and sprawled out on the bench across from where the group was seated. One of them pulled the ear phones out of his ears and sat back against the wall, the music still blaring, as he slurped his soda through the straw. The other sat back in a similar manner and opened a bag of chips.

"What's going on?" one of them said, glancing in Bill's direction.

Bill turned sideways in his chair with no response, as if he didn't hear them.

"Just having a late breakfast and grocery shopping," responded Charlie.

"Well, it's about time I headed home," said Bill, as he raised his body off the chair and got up.

"Yeah, it's about time I headed home too," responded Jack.

With the usual chit chat behind them, the four headed into the mall. Jack and John found a bench to sit on to gawk at the odd assortment of people coming and going.

"Well, I've got to pick up some groceries and catch the bus home," said Charlie. "I'll probably see you tomorrow."

"See you later," replied Jack. John looked up from the newspaper and nodded, as Charlie headed down the mall.

With his shopping completed, Charlie clutched the plastic bag of oranges in his right hand as he walked across the mall entrance to catch the bus.

"Heading home, Charlie?" asked the bus driver, as Charlie deposited the fare in the box.

"There's not much else to do. It's too muggy out. I'm just going to head home and take it easy," responded Charlie.

As the bus driver reached to close the door, the two punks pushed their way through, tossed their fares into the coin meter, and shuffled their way to the rear of the bus.

"If you want to ride on this bus you'd better turn that damn music down. If I have to tell you twice, you'll be walking," yelled the bus driver, turning in his seat and staring at the two.

Charlie exited the bus at his stop, clutching the bag of oranges and groceries in his hand. "Watch your step," said the bus driver, cautioning Charlie as he exited the bus and stepped onto the curb. The two punks pushed up against the side window, staring at Charlie as he made his way up the sidewalk.

"There he goes. Tanya said he lived close by," said one of the punks.

"I wonder what he is going to do today?" stated the other.

"He's probably going home and squeeze some oranges. That's probably the only sex he's seen in twenty years," replied the other punk, laughing and poking his friend on the arm, as the bus pulled past Charlie.

The two stared to see what direction Charlie went as he turned the corner. "I bet the old guy is loaded," one said in a low voice. "Let's get off at the next stop and check it out."

The two got off at the next stop and backtracked. "There he is, up there," said one of the punks, poking the other as they caught sight of Charlie unlocking the front door. After viewing where he lived, the two headed back to the bus stop to catch the bus uptown.

Chapter 3: The Prospectors

The next morning Charlie was up at his usual time. After breakfast, he sat on the folding chair in the entry way, put on his leather work shoes, and headed out to the back yard to throw some leftover bread to the birds.

"Hey Charlie! Come on over and have a seat," came a familiar voice from the yard next door. Charlie's brother Albert, his wife June, and their dog Mac, were sitting on their porch enjoying the morning solitude as they read the newspaper and had a cup of coffee.

"It's going to be another hot one today," said Albert, gazing up as Charlie walked over.

"Yeah, but they call for rain later this evening," replied Charlie.

"What are you up to this morning Charlie?" inquired June.

"I was thinking of going over to Watertown later," responded Charlie.

"Going to the mall?" inquired Albert.

"Just for something to do. Pick up some groceries and have something to eat later. Do you want to go along for the ride?" asked Charlie.

"What time do you think you will be back?" asked Albert, in an excited tone of voice.

"Around 7:00 p.m.," responded Charlie.

"You don't mind if I go with Charlie, do you?" asked Albert, gazing over at June.

"You might as well. All you would do is just sit around here all day moping and driving me crazy," she replied.

"Taking the Chrysler are you?" asked Albert.

"Yeah," responded Charlie. "I'll fill it up with gas in Watertown."

Charlie had the Chrysler parked in the driveway running, when Albert showed up. "All set?" asked Charlie, as he got in.

"Taking the ferry or 401?" asked Albert, shutting the car door behind him, adjusting the seat forward, and fastening his seat belt.

"I'm taking the ferry over. It's shorter and we will get to Watertown faster," replied Charlie. "Maybe 401 on the way back."

Charlie and Albert caught the ferry from Kingston to Wolfe Island. Arriving late, they ended up parking about half way down the length of the ferry surrounded by an assortment of small cars, trucks, and cow trailers. Charlie and Albert got out and stretched their legs. Charlie locked the doors and walked around the car, checking each door several times to make sure it was locked.

After the twenty minute ferry ride, they finally drove off and headed to the other side of the island to catch the boat to Cape Vincent in the U.S.

"The old Chrysler still runs pretty good Charlie," said Albert. "And it's in pretty good shape too. How much do you think it's worth?"

"I just had it appraised for $6,700.00 U.S. dollars," Charlie proudly replied.

"You thinking about selling it?" questioned Albert.

"Not right now. Maybe later," returned Charlie, as they headed down the road and caught the ferry to Cape Vincent and U.S. customs.

Charlie and Albert spent a couple of hours strolling through the Salmon Run Mall, mostly just looking around and checking out prices.

"Hey Charlie, as long as we're here, I think I'll try on some shoes," Albert said, glancing at a pair of shoes in one of the store windows.

"What do you think of these, Charlie?" asked Albert. "They have a full leather sole and lining. Something you don't see very often. And I don't think you can beat the price either."

"They're a good looking shoe. If you bought them in Kingston they would cost nearly twice as much," responded Charlie. "Try a pair on."

"You're right. They're on sale and I don't know when I'll get back over here," said Albert, motioning to the sales person for assistance. "I'd better get a pair now."

With the shopping completed and Albert's purchase of the shoes, they grabbed an early dinner at a buffet style restaurant Charlie usually frequented whenever he was in Watertown.

"That was a pretty good meal and not all that expensive, Charlie. I'll have to bring June here the next time we're over," stated Albert as they walked across the parking lot to the car.

"Which way we headed home, over the bridges to 401 or taking the ferry again?" inquired Albert, as Charlie got onto 81 north.

"It's still early and I thought I'd stop in Clayton. You don't have to get home early, do you?" inquired Charlie.

"No. I'm not in any hurry. Do what you need to do. I'm just enjoying the ride," replied Albert, taking the shoes out of the box and checking them out again.

As Charlie drove into Clayton, he pulled into an older public park, and turned off the car.

"What are we doing here?" asked Albert with a perplexed look.

"Come on, you can help me," replied Charlie, getting out of the car, followed by Albert. Charlie walked to the rear of the Chrysler, opened the trunk and took out a gray, soft covered case.

"What you got there?" asked Albert, still not sure what Charlie was up to.

Charlie unzipped the case and took out several metal parts. In no time at all, he had the parts assembled, and the headphones plugged in, firmly positioned on his head. He adjusted the dials to zero in on metal, other than soda can tops, creating a sequence of high and low pitched tones.

"I thought I would do some metal detecting before it started raining," Charlie said, walking towards the playfield. "Grab the bag and small shovel in the trunk and follow me. I'll show you how this works."

Charlie and Albert spent the next several hours probing the ground from one end of the park to the other. Albert helped carefully dig around the spot wherever they got a hit, as Charlie zeroed in on the precise location of the buried object.

"I think this place has been gone over a lot. There isn't much here," said Charlie. "But we found a few old coins anyway."

"Have you ever found anything worth a lot?" inquired Albert, as Charlie emptied the coins onto the floor of the trunk to examine them.

"Here's one!" exclaimed Charlie, rubbing the dirt off. "It looks like a 1946 American half dollar."

"That's in pretty good shape. What do you think it's worth?" asked Albert.

"Probably only fifty-cents. Once we get home, I can look it up," Charlie replied, putting the coins in a cloth bag.

"It looks like it could start raining any time. I guess we should head home," Charlie said, as he disassembled the metal detector, packed it back in the case, and closed the trunk.

Chapter 4: The Opportunity

Over the next several weeks, Charlie continued to make his usual trips to the mall to kill time and socialize. Tanya saved a seat next to herself each day, anticipating Charlie would be catching the bus to the mall. As Charlie got on the bus, Tanya was talking on her cell phone.

"Ok, he's just getting on. While he's at the mall, you guys check out the house and see if you can find a way in. I'll see if I can find out any more information about his coins. You two geniuses don't exactly fit in the neighborhood, so knock off the weird crap and don't hang around and draw attention to yourselves. Call me later," said Tanya, quickly closing her cell phone and moving her coat to make room for Charlie to sit down.

"Sorry Charlie. I was just talking to one of my girl friends. Don't you look sharp this morning," she said in a flirtatious manner. "I haven't seen you in the last few days. I hope you weren't sick?" inquired Tanya, appearing to be concerned.

"No. I've been feeling ok. I drove my car over to Watertown so it wouldn't be just sitting in one spot all the time. Something different to do. You've got to keep the fluids moving so you don't get any rust," responded Charlie.

After several minutes, Tanya broke the silence. "So Charlie, what is the most valuable coin you've found so far?" Charlie didn't want to talk about his coins, but Tanya ascertained that he had several rare coins worth a lot of money stashed somewhere in the house.

With Charlie at the mall, the two punks walked up both sides of the block past Charlie's house, looking for open windows and an easy area to gain entrance without being noticed. The taller punk, Earl, rang the doorbell to see if anyone answered, while Ray opened the front storm door and turned the knob.

"Locked, with a deadbolt above," said Ray. They proceeded to the side door and rang the doorbell. Ray opened the storm door against the 10 speed bike chained to the side railing and turned the knob. It was also locked. As they turned to walk away, the door opened and a young man, somewhat sleepy-eyed and barefoot, stood in the doorway. "You guys want something?" he asked.

"Ah, just looking to rent a room. Are there any available?" asked Earl.

"No," was the reply as the young man closed the door in their face.

"Well, you don't have to be rude about it!" yelled Earl, stepping off the porch. They continued down the sidewalk, gazing at the rear of the house.

"Hey, over there," said Ray, pointing to a plywood door off the back of the foundation, partially obscured by the overgrown peony plants, a low wooden fence, and wheel barrel.

"Let's go. Give Tanya a call," said Ray, putting his headphones over his ears, and turning up the music.

Tanya glanced at the number on her cell phone as it vibrated several times before picking up.

"Hey, the place is locked up tighter than a bank vault and there's a guy living there," said Ray.

"Yeah, and like he was really rude to us too." interjected Earl. "But I think we found a way in. Do you want us to break-in now?"

"It's broad daylight. Are you two stupid or what?" questioned Tanya. "Charlie won't be home until later tomorrow evening. He's working at some golf course. Let me think about it. I'll call you tomorrow and let you know what I want you to do," directed Tanya, closing her cell phone. "What a couple of idiots," she thought to herself as she sat back in the bar chair, sipping on a margarita, and flirting with an older gentleman, unaware of her intentions.

The next morning, Tanya called Ray to go over the details of the plan. "Charlie won't be home until around 10:00 tonight. You two check out the house as soon as it gets dark and make sure no one is home. And see if the guy upstairs is there. It's a Saturday night, so he should be out late partying with his friends.

"Well, don't worry, if he's there, I'll take care of him," said Earl.

"Smarten up Earl. You just get in, find the coins, and get out. Got it?" stated Tanya in a forceful tone. "You won't have time to mess around, so you need to look everywhere, behind everything, and pull out drawers. The money is hidden somewhere. Try to dress to fit into the neighborhood. And for God's sake, wear gloves, and keep the damn music turned off so you can hear if anyone comes in. Call me back when you find the coins," she concluded, flipping her cell phone shut.

Once it was dark, Earl and Ray met down the block from the house to discuss strategy. Ray walked past the house to see if he saw any movement inside. Several lights were on throughout the first floor, but the second floor was dark. It didn't appear anyone was home.

Earl walked around the side and noticed the 10 speed bike still chained to the railing. He pulled out his box cutter and slit both the front and rear tires. "That'll teach the asshole to be disrespectful," he said, closing the cutter and putting it back in his pocket.

Earl caught up with Ray at the end of the property line. They squeezed through the opening at the end of the wooden fence to gain access to the backyard. After crawling along the stone planting wall they reached the location of the plywood door to the cellar. Ray stepped around the wheel barrel and hoses to position himself in front of the door. Earl handed him the small pry bar which he wedged under the lock and pushed the door inward and open.

"You go up the steps and check out the first floor. I'll check out the cellar," whispered Ray as he closed the door behind him.

There weren't any windows in the cellar, so Ray turned on his flashlight and started going through the pile of boxes. Earl headed up the steps to check out the first floor, but soon came back down.

"Hey Ray, the door is locked from the first floor. What now?" inquired Earl.

"Here, you look in the cellar. I'll open the door and check out the first floor," stated Ray. Reaching the top of the steps, Ray put his ear against the space along the edge of the door for several minutes to listen. Confident nobody was home, he pushed the flat end of the pry bar between the door and the frame and pushed on the door with his shoulder.

The cracking sound of wood was momentary. The door flew open as Ray leaned against the frame to keep from falling into the room. He waited to see if anyone heard the noise before moving. Everything was quiet.

Ray closed the cellar door, but not completely, and unlocked the one next to it. He slowly opened the door and peered into the connecting hallway to the side entrance that provided access to the second floor. Ray shut the door, locked it again, and began checking out the rooms, careful to stay away from the windows and lights.

"God it's hot and muggy in here. Doesn't this guy believe in air conditioning?" Ray thought, as he started going through Charlie's bedroom. He pulled out the dresser drawers and rummaged through their content, looking behind the dresser and bed, and poking around the closet shelves.

"Hum? Nothing in here. Man, I can't breathe in this place," he said to himself, as he put the drawers back in the dresser and got out of the room.

Ray went through the living room, kitchen, and finally the bathroom. He pulled out every drawer and appliance. Still nothing.

"Hey Earl, you find anything?" inquired Ray, stepping halfway down the cellar stairs and yelling in a low voice.

"Nah. There's nothing down here. Give Tanya a call and let's get out of here," responded Earl coming up the steps.

As the two moved into the living room, the headlights from Charlie's 65 Chrysler highlighted the bedroom blinds and spread out onto the walls. The sound of the garage door opening further raised the rush of adrenalin through Ray and Earl.

"The old guy's home early. Let's get out of here," said Earl, as he proceeded towards the cellar steps.

"Hold on. As soon as he sees the damage to the door, he'll be calling the cops. The money is here somewhere, and we're not leaving until we have what we came for. Here, put this hood on and get in the bedroom closet. And keep your mouth shut. I'll take care of Charlie," stated Ray.

"What do you mean take care of? Call Tanya and ask her what we should do," insisted Earl.

"Put the damn hood on and get in the F'n closet. I'm not going to hurt the old guy unless he doesn't want to cooperate. Then that's a different story," responded Ray.

Chapter 5: Heavy Metal

Charlie pulled into the garage, turned the car ignition off, and closed the garage door behind him. Ray edged himself tight to the wall behind the bathroom door as Charlie opened the door between the garage and the front entry.

"Oh boy. It's been a long day," Charlie said to himself, taking off his hat and sitting down on the metal folding chair to remove his shoes. Charlie ran his hand through his hair as he got up and walked into the kitchen. He opened the refrigerator, grabbed a cold Molson beer, and took a drink to relieve the day's heat. As he headed to the bathroom to urinate, he noticed the cellar door partially open and the wood casing cracked.

"Anyone here?" yelled Charlie, in a loud voice, as he moved backwards into the kitchen to turn on the light and call the police. As Charlie picked up the phone and began dialing, Ray came up behind him, ripped the cord from the wall, and pushed Charlie against the refrigerator.

"Who you calling Charlie, the cops? Do exactly as I tell you and nobody needs to get hurt. Now sit down and shut up," ordered Ray, grabbing Charlie by the arm and pushing him into the kitchen chair. "Here, finish your beer," said Ray, slamming the can on the kitchen table.

Earl peered around the wall to the kitchen to make sure everything was under control before he came in.

"Who are you? What do you want?" questioned Charlie as he sat in the chair, rubbing his bruised arm.

"Shut up," ordered Ray. "I'll do the talking. You just listen and do as you're told."

"Get some towels, tie him up, and blindfold him," Ray directed, motioning to Earl.

"Why do I have do blind fold him Ray, why don't...."

"Shut up. Just shut the F' up!" exclaimed Ray, cutting Earl short and jerking him to the other side of the kitchen. "I told you no names. Where's your head, huh?"

"Ok. This is how it's going to work. We ask you a question and if you give us the correct answer, you won't get hurt. But if you mess with us, that bruise on your arm is going to get a lot bigger. Understand?" stated Ray, in a soothing tone in Charlie's ear.

"Ok, where are the coins?" asked Ray.

"What coins?" Charlie replied back in a firm voice.

"Now, remember what I told you Charlie? If you don't give me what I want, I'll have to hurt you," responded Ray.

"Hey, she never said anything about hurting him," blurted Earl.

"What did I tell you about keeping you're damn mouth shut? Keep your damn mouth shut. Got it?" responded Ray, clenching his teeth and glaring over at Earl.

"Ok, let's try again. Where are the coins? The ones you found with your metal detector that are supposed to be worth a lot of money. I know they're hidden somewhere in the house," Ray said again, smacking Charlie against the side of the head.

"They're in a case on the table in the living room, off the side entrance," responded Charlie.

"Go check it out," Ray ordered and motioned to Earl.

Earl opened the door to the side entrance hallway and turned the knob to open the living room door. "It's locked," replied Earl.

"Where's the key?" asked Ray.

"In my front pants pocket," responded Charlie.

Ray reached into Charlie's front pocket and pulled out a key chain. "What the hell is this? There's got to be at least 20 keys on this thing," stated Ray.

"Here, find the right key and open the door," Ray said, throwing the key chain to Earl. Earl fumbled with the keys, trying each one in the lock.

"Come on. Speed it up," blurted Ray.

"I'm working on it. The damn door has two different locks. You come and do it if you think it's so easy," responded Earl in frustration.

Earl continued until he found the keys to open the door. "Yeah, just my luck, it would have to be the last key I try," mumbled Earl, turning the knob and opening the door.

The hallway light partially illuminated the otherwise dark interior of the room. Earl turned on the lights and grabbed the metal case sitting on the coffee table. "Got It," he said, trying to pick it up with one hand.

"Boy is this thing heavy," he blurted out, as the case fell to the floor. Earl bent down, grabbed the case with both hands, and started back to the kitchen, stopping several times to let his arms rest.

"Hey, turn off the lights and shut the doors," Ray motioned.

As Earl plopped the briefcase on the kitchen table, the side entrance door opened and slammed shut. "Damn it. What the F'!" came the angry and emotional words from the college student just returning. Ray and Earl stood silent as they heard knocking on the inner door.

"Charlie, you home? Charlie? Someone slashed my bike tires." After several seconds, they heard the student's footsteps going up the stairs to the second floor. Ray grabbed a knife from the drawer and started to pry the locks open when he was interrupted by footsteps coming back down the stairs. Their attention was focused on the inner door, as a piece of paper was slid under it.

"Charlie? Are you home? You left the living room door open?"

Earl and Ray remained silent until they heard the student return to his room on the second floor.

"Want me to get it?" asked Earl.

"Yeah Earl. Why don't you run over there and get the damn piece of paper so the guy upstairs can hear you. Smarten up," said Ray, inserting the knife under the locks and snapping them open.

"Easy as cake. What are you going to do with your share?" Earl whispered.

"I haven't thought about it," answered Ray.

"I'm getting a tattoo on the back of my neck," replied Earl.

Ray opened the top with anticipated excitement to gaze at the coins. "What the F' is this?" blurted Ray in astonishment, staring at a conglomeration of melted metal formed in the shape of a cube.

"Where are the coins?" whispered Earl, looking at Ray straight in the face.

"Ok Charlie, what are you trying to pull. Where are the coins?" whispered Ray, as he leaned against Charlie's ear.

"They're the coins. You're looking at them. I don't know what other coins you think I have," returned Charlie.

"The ones you said are worth a lot of money," responded Ray.

"They're all the coins I have. They're pure silver and worth a lot. I have them all itemized. The list should be in the box with the coins," responded Charlie.

Ray grabbed the piece of paper and looked at the hand written list of coins and their value. "There's supposed to be over $120,000 in coins, but all I see is melted metal," stated Ray.

"Wait a minute," interjected Earl, examining the metal closer. "These are coins, or what's left of them. They've just been melted together."

Ray hit his hand against the refrigerator in disgust. "What the F. What are you, nuts? You melted them? All this amounts to is just a worthless piece of metal." said Ray.

"You'd better get her on the phone and find out what she wants us to do now," Earl said, in an anxious tone of voice.

"Just shut up a minute," returned Ray, listening to the student coming down the stairs again.

"Charlie? Charlie? Are you ok?" questioned the student, as he repeatedly knocked on the door. "I called the police about my bike and they want to talk to you."

Chapter 6: Caller ID

Ray and Earl stood silent. "Leave this stuff and let's get out of here before the cops show up," whispered Earl nervously. Earl and Ray started towards the cellar door, but halfway across the living room Ray's cell phone rang. "Oh shit!" exclaimed Ray, reaching into his pocket to turn it off. Earl and Ray stared at the door knob as the student repeatedly turned and pulled at it.

"Charlie, what's going on? Are you ok?"

Ray and Earl made a dash to the cellar door and down the stairs.

"Ok, you two, hold it right there," came a voice as Ray and Earl made their way out through the plywood door to the back yard. The police had responded to the student's call, and were in the process of checking the house when they observed Earl and Ray exiting the cellar.

Charlie's brother Albert had noticed the police cars and walked up to the house to see what was going on. He used his key to open the front entrance door and gain access to the house.

Albert and the police found Charlie blindfolded and tied up in the kitchen, and the glob of metal on the table.

"Hey Charlie, are you ok? What's all this stuff? They didn't get your coin collection, did they?" asked Albert, removing the blindfold and untying him.

"I'm ok. Just a little bruised. My son has the coin collection," responded Charlie.

"We caught the two trying to get out of the cellar. We're bringing them around now so you can identify them," stated the police officer.

The police made out their report and Charlie identified the two punks from Wal-Mart before they were taken downtown to be booked. The calls on Ray's cell phone lead the police to Tanya as an accomplice in the scheme.

The following morning Charlie caught the bus as usual. Tanya wasn't expecting to see him and was startled. "Charlie. What a surprise?" she gasped, as Charlie sat down beside her. "Headed to the Mall?"

"No, I have to go downtown to complete some paperwork. I don't think we will be seeing much of each other after this morning," responded Charlie, glancing over at her.

"What do you mean Charlie? Are you going away?" returned Tanya.

"No, I believe you are," responded Charlie with a smile, slowly rising from his seat as the bus pulled up to the mall entrance. Tanya looked at at Charlie as to question what he meant, when she noticed two police officers getting on the bus.

Charlie brushed past the two officers as he exited the front of the bus. He stood alone on the sidewalk next to the window where Tanya was seated, smiling and waving a final goodbye, as he watched the police take her into custody.

The End

Beyond Reasonable Doubt

3

Former CIA agent Ray Darby, recently deployed to the U.S. Airbase in Taiwan, thought it was just a simple problem when the Ford F150 he was issued didn't start. Repeated disruptions in the truck's electrical system and increased occurrences of power, communications, and military hardware failures, coincided with several unannounced satellite launches by the Chinese government.

With the help of his long time friend Jack Walsh at Bell Labs, they uncover a scheme of deceptive manufacturing by the Chinese that could leave the U.S. military and its allies impotent. With no time to spare, the U.S. must counter the threat that could leave its allies in Southeast Asia vulnerable to a nuclear confrontation.

Chapter 1: The Commitment

Thursday, 1730 hours, 25°N, 120°E, the Taiwan Strait. Sky clear, visibility 7 miles, temperature 87 deg., water condition calm.

The blast of the high-pressure steam from the ship's reactors and engine thrust, against the jet blast deflector, slammed the F/A-18 fighter forward and catapulted it from the flight deck into the air from 0 to 165 miles per hour in two seconds. The exhilarating rush was felt by the flight crews, scrambling to position themselves as aircraft landed and took off at a furious rate throughout the day and into the evening.

The aircraft carrier USS Nimitz, encompassing the Commander Strike Group, Commander Destroyer Strike Group, and the Command Carrier Air Wing has been deployed in the East China Sea to patrol the air space along the coast of Taiwan, up the coast of Japan, and over the Korean peninsula. The build-up of the U.S. military was in direct response to its commitment to defend the island in the wake of renewed threats of hostility from mainland China and the growing tension over nuclear tests by North Korea.

In a show of ongoing cooperation efforts in the Pacific region, the U.S. navy is joined by the 3rd/427th Tactical Fighter Wing (TFW) from Ching Chuan Kang AB with three squadrons of air defense/attack fighters and support from the army's airborne and special operations' command. The air base's intelligence and security agencies interface and provide additional early warning air defense to detect and intercept enemy aircraft. Additional TFW aircraft from Hsinchu,

Taoyuan, Tainan, Chiaya, and Pingtung Air Bases have been deployed to support the mission.

Throughout the day, the returning aircraft stacked up in an oval flying pattern around the carrier. As the landing signal officer guided them in, they broke free of the landing patterns and lined up with the stern of the carrier and the landing guidance lights for their approach. As soon as the aircraft hit the deck, the tailhook snagged one of the arresting wires stretched across the flight deck as the pilot pushed the engines to full power in case he needed to take off again and come around for another pass. As the hydraulic cylinders absorbed the energy from the aircraft, it came to an abrupt stop within 2-seconds in the 315-foot landing area.

"Another one down!" exclaimed the Air Boss, directing the aircraft activity from the Command Center Operations, six stories above the flight deck. "How many still out?" he questioned, glancing at the Mini Boss, his assistant.

"Two," responded the Mini Boss, reaching for the phone. "Flight Control, Captain Halsey," he answered.

"Sir, Air Traffic Control just lost communications with two aircraft, 17 miles out. They're trying to make contact but there's a lot of interference. Intelligence surveillance confirms no hostile aircraft in the area," reported the Mini Boss, still clutching the phone against his ear, engaging with Air Traffic Control.

"Keep trying to reach them. Get the Combat Direction Center on the horn and have them stand by, ordered the Air Boss, brushing past the command center doorway from outside the observation deck.

After several moments, the silence was broken. "ATC has contact, but it's garbled and barely discernable. They're 12-miles out and…Sir! ACT has just lost one aircraft from the scope," blurted the Mini Boss, glaring at the Air Boss for direction.

"Scramble two fighters and get a chopper in the air," ordered the Air Boss, picking up the phone to notify the Strike Group Commander of the situation.

"Sir, ATC has voice contact with one of the pilots, 7-miles out and setting up to land. He's reporting intermittent engine and electrical failure. The other pilot ejected and is in the water awaiting rescue," reported the Mini Boss.

"Have a fire truck stand by on the flight deck and the crash barricade in place," ordered the Air Boss, walking onto the outside observation deck to make visual contact with the approaching F/A-18 aircraft.

"There he is!" exclaimed the Mini Boss, pointing in the direction of the approaching aircraft, as its light faintly illuminated the evening sky.

"He's coming in too low," yelled the Air Boss, taking the phone from the Mini Boss to communicate with ATC. After several intense moments, as the aircraft continued to lose altitude and skim above the water surface, it suddenly gained altitude and lined up with the landing guidance lights. Its tailhook missed the fourth arresting wire as the aircraft's engines shut down and it came to a stop in the crash barricade netting stretched across the flight deck.

"Sir," voiced the Mini Boss, hanging up the phone. "Search and rescue aircraft have located the downed pilot in the water and marked his position for pickup. The pilot has given us the thumbs up."

"As soon as the pilots are checked out, notify me and have them report to the debriefing room We need to find out what happed up there and how in the hell we lost a plane," stated the Air Boss in a rushed tone, heading down the observation deck stairway.

Chapter 2: Country Roads

The morning heat had the sweat running down the side of Ray's face as he pulled his leather gloves tight to his fingers. He wrapped his hands around the baling twine, grabbing onto the hay bale. With one continuous motion, he swung the bale high, releasing it as his arms were pulled outward from the momentum, throwing it onto the flatbed trailer. His younger brother Jim took over and stacked it squarely among the bales.

"Ok," yelled Ray, as his father pulled the Ford pickup forward to the remaining bales.

"Man, I'm beat!" Jim blurted out, sliding off the pile of bales and onto the ground.

"You think you're tired!" exclaimed Ray. "Tomorrow you can throw them on the trailer and I'll stack them. I'm the one that's supposed to be on vacation," he said, pulling his tee shirt out from inside his pants and wiping the sweat from his eyes.

"Ok you two, get in. You'd think you were done for the day. The hay isn't going to unload itself," responded their father, leaning to the side and opening the passenger door, while continuing to drive forward. Jim jumped in, followed by Ray, grabbing onto the handle at the truck interior and pulling himself in.

"We'll unload the hay before lunch and call it a day," said their father, as he sped up and headed across the pasture and down the dirt road to the horse stable.

Ray was barely out of the truck when Jim pushed past him and climbed up the vertical wall of hay bales to reach the top.

"Just don't stand there, get your ass in gear," Jim yelled to Ray, as he began tossing the bales off the trailer.

"Hey, quit making a mess of everything. Wait until I catch up," yelled Ray, scrambling to try to stay ahead of the constant barrage of bales being thrown at his feet.

"I'll be in the paddock brushing the mare down. When you two are done fooling around, unhook the truck and I'll meet you back at the house," stated their father, heading towards the stable.

With the hay stacked, Jim started the truck as Ray unhooked the trailer. "Ok, let's move it. Time to eat," yelled Ray, jumping in the box and pounding on the wheel-well fender. Jim hit the gas, leaving a trail of dust behind them, and headed to the house.

"You boys wash up before you have lunch. And that goes for you too, dad. We've got company," said their mother Edna, carrying a plate of salmon sandwiches and a pitcher of ice lemonade out to the front porch.

"Dad, you bring the plate of fruit on the table with you when you come," Edna yelled back.

Ray pushed his tee shirt back into his pants to look somewhat presentable before opening the porch screen door. Friends of the family, Maggie and Carl, had stopped in to say hi, but found themselves staying for lunch at Edna's insistence.

"Welcome back home," said Carl, getting up from the wicker chair to shake Ray's hand.

Maggie scurried behind Edna's chair and gave Ray a hug and quick kiss on the cheek. "Edna told us you were home on vacation, but by the looks of it, your father has been putting you to work," she said in a raised voice, turning her head and staring over at Frank.

"He's got the easy work. I'm doing all the hard stuff," responded Jim, with his mouth full from a bite of the sandwich.

"Oh yeah, that will be the day," replied Edna, pouring a glass of lemonade.

"How long are you home for Ray, or should I say, Major Darby, Sir?" inquired Carl, snapping to attention.

"One more week," responded Ray with a chuckle.

"Then guess where they're sending him? Of all the places on this earth, they're sending him off to some air base in Taiwan. That's the next trouble spot we're going to find ourselves defending. You mark my words," interjected Edna.

"Are you still with Navy intelligence?" inquired Maggie.

"Yes, and it's not as bad as my mother projects it to be. I'm hoping to be over there no more than 12-months..." stated Ray, but was cut short by a tug at his pant leg and two loud barks.

"Hey girlfriend," he said in an excited tone, turning and kneeling down to greet Cody, Maggie and Carl's three-year old chocolate lab. "I haven't forgotten you. You're still the best looking girl I know," replied Ray, scratching her behind the ears and giving her a big kiss on the nose.

"I think Ray's in love," said Jim, scooping up another sandwich.

No sooner had Ray sat down beside Maggie when Cody put her front paws on his lap and pushed her nose under his arm, insisting on being the center of attention.

"I believe our love is mutual," interjected Ray, staring into her big brown eyes and giving her a hug.

"Ok, you two. You can make out later. You better get something to eat before your brother devours everything," demanded Edna, pushing the remaining sandwiches closer to Ray.

"And they're for you, not Cody," insisted Carl.

"Cody hasn't had any puppies yet?" asked Ray.

"Well, since you brought it up, I'm afraid there's another man in her life right now besides you. She has been courting a handsome chocolate male that's pretty interested in her. We'll just have to wait and see what develops," replied Maggie.

"Why you little two-timer!" responded Ray. "If you have puppies, you better save me one."

"Oh, I don't think Cody would let them all go without saving you the pick of the litter," returned Maggie.

The get together and reminiscing continued into the mid-afternoon before Maggie, Carl, and Cody had to head home. As the days counted down, Ray was able to find some time to relax and catch up on some overdue reading. He met up with a few friends at Molly Darcy's Pub to down a few beers, listen to some music, and talk about old times. But staying home and spending time with his aging parents and younger brother was more of a priority for him; especially since his stay was short.

In the meantime, Ray helped his father take care of the horses and do other odd chores around the horse farm, located just north of Danbury, Connecticut. Of course, his brother's daily taunting, which usually came out of left field and usually caught Ray off-guard, livened up his daily routine. On more than one occasion, Ray's mother attempted to forcefully evict him from the house when he insisted on helping her clean. But when all was said and done, he ended up helping anyway, despite her loud protests.

The day everyone kept trying to avoid thinking about finally arrived as Ray's vacation time came to an end. While Ray helped his brother finish off the home cooked breakfast, Frank loaded his luggage into the car trunk.

"Ok, let's get a move-on," Frank said, standing outside the porch door, gazing at his watch, and motioning everyone out to the car.

"Frank, it's only 5:30 in the morning. You're always in a rush," responded Edna.

"I'm not taking any chances on Ray missing his flight. You know how long some of those lines at security can be," blurted Frank.

With everyone ready, Frank drove to the end of the driveway, stopped, and opened the car door to get out.

"For God's sake, now what are you doing?" inquired Edna.

"Just hold your horses. I'm going to grab the morning paper," responded Frank.

"Well, put a rush on it. We don't want Ray to miss his flight to D.C. We only have 2-hours to get to the airport," returned Edna, catching the newspaper in her lap.

"Here, this will keep you quiet for a while," Frank said, with no attempt to keep back his laughter.

The ride to the airport was calm and relaxing, that is until Edna opened the newspaper. "Just look at the headlines," gasped Edna, holding up the Danbury News Times and pointing to an article buried on page 4A. *"Joint Military Maneuvers with Taiwan Increase U.S.-Chinese Tensions.'* It says that in an attempt to intimidate Taiwan, China intends to conduct missile tests and concurrent joint military exercises close to Taiwan."

"Mom, there's nothing to get worked up about. If it was a national concern, the newspaper would have printed it on the front page, not burry it somewhere in the middle," Ray said in a low whisper, resting his hand on her shoulder to console Edna.

"You're telling me there's nothing to worry about?" interrupted Edna in a firm tone of voice. "Frank, you turn this damn car around." But Frank just ignored Edna, as usual, and kept driving.

"Ok, I'm going to drop you off at the curb so you can get in and get your tickets. I'll park the car and meet you inside," Frank said, approaching the terminal drop off zone.

After Ray picked up his airline tickets, Frank caught up with them as they were headed to airport security screening. "My God, look at the line of people. I'm glad we left two hours early, just to get here and wait in line until they open," stated Edna in bewilderment, glancing in Frank's direction.

"Ok, you two. So we're a little early," responded Ray. "It gives us more time together."

Ray's imminent departure hit his younger brother Jim the hardest, though he tried not to show it. "Hey, I'll see you in less than a year. You take care and stay out of trouble. I'll keep in touch by e-mail with you," Ray said, giving Jim a firm hug.

"You too," replied Jim. "I think I'll take mom and dad out for Chinese tonight. What do you think?"

"I think you should maybe rethink that and take them to Outback instead," responded Ray.

"I'll be staying with Jack and Renee in Alexandria for a couple of days until I catch my flight to Taiwan. I'll call you when I get there. Love you both," Ray said, giving his father and mother a hug and kiss before heading through airport security, occasionally looking back and waving to everyone.

"I'll be home in less than a year," Ray yelled back, smiling and waving, trying to hold back the tears.

Chapter 3: Monday Morning (Sure Looks Fine)

"In this morning's headline news, Congress continues locked in bitter debate over the President's refusal to extend the 'Most Favored Trade' status to China. This, in the wake of renewed tensions between China and the United States over Taiwan and the covert and unannounced launching of a satellite last week by China. More on this, we turn live to....."

Arriving in Taiwan, Major Darby took up residence in the military housing development near Ching Chuan Kang AB. Ray hit the off button on the radio. "0600 hours already, just another 10 minutes," he said to himself in a low agonizing tone of voice, rolling over to get out of bed.

After a quick shower and breakfast, he grabbed his cup of coffee and headed out the door for the drive to the U.S. base. The lingering odor in the morning breeze brought back unforgettable memories, as he paused to reminisce about his adventures wandering through China Town, in lower Manhattan, with his parents when he was younger.

After another sip of coffee, he tossed his briefcase onto the front seat of the government issued Ford F150, put the key in the ignition, and started the truck. Click, click, click. The engine wouldn't turn over. Ray cranked the engine repeatedly.

"What the hell now?" Ray said in a disgusted voice. He turned the key again, pushed the gas peddle all the way to the floor and cranked. Still nothing. The gas gauge was barely above empty, but still enough fuel to make it to the base. Ray pulled the hood latch and climbed out, opened the hood, and checked the battery connections and spark plug wires.

Satisfied that everything looked and felt normal, he jumped back in and tried starting the truck again. Still nothing. Opening the glove compartment, he reached in and pulled out the owner's manual to locate the fuses. After reading through the list of fuses that could be the problem, Ray crawled under the front dash and popped the cover on the fuse box to check to see if any had blown. Everything checked out.

Totally annoyed with the situation, he grabbed for his cell phone and telephoned the base motor pool for assistance.

"Motor Pool, Sergeant Marko speaking. May I help you?" was the man's voice on the other end.

"Yes. This is Major Darby, my Ford F150 won't start." After qualifying all of the particular information and confirming he was in a safe location, Sergeant Marko informed him that a tow truck would be there as soon as possible. Ray pulled the key out of the ignition and was about to get out when Major Karen Morrissey jogged up the driveway with a perplexed look.

"You haven't left for the base?" she inquired.

"The damn truck won't start," replied Ray, slamming the front hood down.

"What? You just got it. Do you need a ride to the base?" she asked.

"No," responded Ray. "I called the motor pool and they're sending a tow truck."

"Well, with all the vehicles you had to choose from, it was your decision to get a Ford," said Karen, moving closer, with her body against his, trying to look interested in the problem at hand.

"You can't fix it? I thought all guys knew how to fix trucks," Karen said in a teasing tone.

"Did anyone ever tell you you're annoying?" questioned Ray with a smile, as he leaned over and quickly kissed her on the lips.

"No. You're the first," responded Karen, returning the smile and making eye contact with Ray.

"God! What kind of perfume do you wear? My eyes are starting to burn," said Ray, looking at her as he shut both eyes.

"I'm not wearing... Oh. Don't rub your eyes. That's pepper spray. I wanted to see what it smelled like and accidentally sprayed some on my tee shirt. Sorry," responded Karen, returning the kiss on Ray's cheek. "Good luck with your truck. Maybe I'll see you later," she yelled back, as she took off jogging back to her apartment.

The tow truck finally arrived a short time later and loaded the Ford onto the back of the flat bed. Ray climbed in the front seat, buckled his seat belt, and looked at the driver in a frustrated manner. "Doesn't anything you buy today work properly?" Ray asked sarcastically.

The driver towed the truck to the base motor pool garage and unloaded it in the back lot. Ray thought about the situation as he walked to the truck. Maybe it didn't start because it was low on fuel and parked at an angle in the driveway. Loading the truck on a level flatbed redistributed the gas.

"Just one last try," Ray thought. He got in, pushed the key into the ignition, and turned. It started. Excited, he hit the steering wheel with both hands. "Yes!" Ray turned the truck off and turned the ignition again. It started again. "Yeah," said Ray. "That must have been it."

After notifying the private at the service desk, Ray headed to work, but not before filling up with fuel.

"Where were you this morning?" was the usual question from base personnel as Ray arrived at the office two hours late.

"My truck wouldn't start," responded Ray.

"I thought you had a new truck?" came a man's voice from behind a low workstation wall.

"You got it," was Ray's response.

"Well, you know what they say about Fords?" was the response back.

"Yeah, I know," interjected Ray before he had a chance to finish this statement.

The work day seemed longer than usual, but finally ended. As Ray headed out the door and walked to his truck, he wondered if the it would start again. It did as he sighed with relief.

Chapter 4: Tuesday (I've Got Traveling on My Mind)

Ray had turned in early the night before to prepare for an early morning staff briefing. Before his alarm could go off, Ray was awakened by Major Morrissey's voice from the driveway below.

"Hey Ray, are you going to sleep all morning?" she yelled out with a childish, prodding tone in her voice, as she prepared to go jogging.

"Thanks for the wakeup," Ray said as he looked out the bedroom window at Karen. "God she's cute," Ray thought to himself.

After a quick shower and breakfast, Ray headed out the door. Unlocking the truck, he placed his coffee cup in the holder between the seats, tossed his briefcase in, and prepared for the drive to pick up Col. Evans and catch their flight to Pingtung Air Base for a meeting.

Click, Click. Nothing. "Not again! What in the hell is going on here?" Ray yelled in a disgusted voice. "This can't be happening." He turned the key in the ignition and cranked the engine repeatedly. Still nothing. Ray grabbed his cell phone and telephoned Col. Evans to advise him of the situation.

"Not again?" was the response on the other end. "You have the motor pool pick up that truck. And see if they have a bicycle you can use," responded the Colonel. "I'll attend the meeting. When you get to the office, you can log into the teleconference at 0800. If you can't make it…"

"Hello? Col. Evans? What the hell!" Ray blurted out in a disgusted tone.

"Now what?" responded Major Morrissey, making her way up the driveway.

"The truck won't start and now the damn cell phone just went dead. What a piece of junk. Doesn't anything work around here?"

Ray hit the End button on the cell phone until it turned on again and called the base motor pool for a tow. Around 0700 the tow truck arrived. As it backed into the driveway, Ray was relieved that it was a different driver from the previous day. He didn't know how he would have handled the intimidation of the same thing happening two days in a row.

The truck was loaded and hauled to the base motor pool. After unloading it in the back parking lot, Ray was reluctant to even hope the truck would start, but he got in and turned the ignition. Click, Click. It wouldn't start this time. Confident the motor pool would be able to run a diagnostic on the electrical and fuel systems and have it repaired by the end of the day, Ray got a ride to the office from the garage shuttle service.

At mid morning Ray received a telephone call from the Sergeant Marko at the garage. "We just pulled your truck in. Did you try starting the truck with a different key?" inquired Sergeant Marko.

"No," responded Ray. "I'm the only person who drives the truck and I use the key I have always used. Why?"

"It sounds like a problem with the anti-theft system. We're swamped here this morning, but I'll try to get to it as soon as I can and give you a call when it's ready. If we can't get to it, I'll get you another truck to use until we figure this out," responded Sergeant Marko.

As 1600 hours approached the telephone rang. "This is Sergeant Marko over at the motor pool. Your truck is ready. We'll send a driver over to pick you up."

Arriving at the motor pool, Ray asked what the problem was.

"We had to replace the battery," said the Private at the service desk. "It tested weak."

"What?" said Ray, with a puzzled look on his face. "You replaced the battery?"

"Everything else checked out," was the Private's reply.

"That's ridiculous," said Ray. "The engine cranked trying to start and didn't show any signs of being weak."

"Well, that's what we came up with," was the reply from the Private. "If you need to discuss it, you'll have to wait until tomorrow morning when Sergeant Marko gets in."

Climbing into the truck, Ray turned the key. The truck started. Lacking confidence that the battery was the problem, he turned the truck off and on again several times. Assured that it would start, he pulled out of the motor pool parking lot and headed back to the office.

Chapter 5: Wednesday (I've Got My Doubts)

"Topping this morning's news, the U.S. Pentagon is further monitoring the position of the satellite launched early last week by the Chinese government. The Chinese, however, have not acknowledged the launch.

In other developments, the FBI has confirmed that the engineers at Bell Laboratories, in cooperation with coordinated international efforts, played a crucial part leading to the detection and breakup of a European botnet scheme last week. Authorities say six men were arrested in connection with a scheme in which hundreds of thousands of computers where allegedly infected with a malicious computer code and then used as zombie PC's to commit additional crimes. According to authorities, an estimated 315,000 compromised computers, running under a common command-and-control infrastructure, were capable of sending over 60 billion spam messages a day."

"Bell Labs, huh. I bet Jack had something to do with it," Ray thought as he hit the off button on the television remote and headed out the door with a hot cup of coffee and briefcase in hand. Major Morrissey was usually half way through her jogging, but decided to wait around to see if the truck would start, or at least to offer support if it didn't. Not confident that the truck would start, Ray pulled out his cell phone as he climbed in and turned the ignition. Click, Click.

"This damn piece of junk!" Ray yelled, pounding the steering wheel with both fists. "I told those idiots at the motor pool it wasn't the battery." Ray pushed the gas peddle to the floor and cranked the engine repeatedly.

"Don't get worked up," responded Major Morrissey, trying hard to keep the grin on her face from showing.

The truck still wouldn't start. After placing another call to motor pool, the truck was towed to the service garage and Ray got a ride to the office again, only this time with Major Morrissey.

By mid afternoon Ray received the awaited call from the motor pool informing him that the anti-theft sensor went south. Unfortunately they didn't have a replacement part in stock and had to order one. That meant the truck wouldn't be ready until the following day, or possibly even longer.

"Fine, just fine!" Ray blurted out in a disgusted voice, as he hung up the telephone. Turning to continue work, he glanced up to notice Major Morrissey, standing by his door.

"Need a ride to pick up your truck?" she asked.

"Thanks, but it won't be ready until tomorrow. They said something about having to order an anti-theft module for the ignition. But I could use a ride home," replied Ray.

"Sure," responded Major Morrissey. "See you in the lobby at 1600 hours."

"They sure don't make cars like they use to," said Ray, as he and Major Morrissey walked across the parking lot to her car.

"Yeah," responded Major Morrissey. "It's really weird. You sure have had a lot of problems with that truck all of a sudden. It's like a James Bond movie. Maybe a covert foreign agent is messing with your truck's electrical system while you're sleeping," she said jokingly.

"You may have a point. People say I do look a lot like James Bond," responded Ray, opening the car door for Karen.

"Yeah, right! Get in James Bond. I'll drive you home. I certainly wouldn't want the responsibility for the security of the free world on my shoulders if anything happens to you," said Major Morrissey with a smile that spread across her face. "But let's stop and grab a bite. I found the greatest French restaurant that serves the best escargot. My treat."

"You've got to be kidding. No way!" said Ray, as a sick look overtook him. "A burger and a cold beer. My treat," he fired back, jumping in the driver's seat. "And I'll drive."

The part was sent over-night delivery from the U.S. base in Japan, but Ray wasn't able to pick up the truck for several more days. That gave him the opportunity spend more time with Major Morrissey.

Arriving at the motor pool garage he headed over to the service desk to pick up his keys. "You're all set. Looks like the anti-theft module for the ignition was defective," said the Private at the desk. "Sorry it took so long, but yours wasn't the only vehicle with problems. We've been swamped over the last couple of months with similar problems. That's why we couldn't get to your vehicle sooner."

"Say that again?" responded Ray. "No one said anything to me about other vehicles with the same type of problems when I had the truck towed here before. And it took three times before you figured out the problem and fixed it? Unbelievable!" exclaimed Ray.

"We get to them when we can. But that's nothing. Everything seems to be breaking down lately," responded the Private, pointing to the clip board on the desk behind him filled with work orders.

"Hum," said Ray. "My cell phone has been going dead a lot lately. Major Morrissey said something about having problems with her cell phone going dead and then just turning back on again. And then there are the problems with the vehicles. I really never gave it much thought. Strange."

Ray picked up his keys to leave, but stopped short. "You wouldn't still have that module would you?" inquired Ray.

"Maybe. See the guy over there," said the Private, pointing to one of the garage mechanics.

Ray headed over to the mechanic and inquired about the module. "Do you still have the module for the Ford pickup you replaced?" asked Ray.

"Possibly. Why, do you want it? There's nothing to look at except a piece of plastic," said the mechanic.

"Yes, if you have it," responded Ray.

After rummaging through the pile of parts on his work bench, the mechanic found the module. "Here it is," said the mechanic, handing it to Ray. "I remember when everything used to be made in Japan. Nowadays it seems that everything is made in China or some other third world country. Nothing but junk if you ask me."

"Thanks," responded Ray, slipping it into his coat pocket.

Chapter 6: Sleepless Nights (Transponder 101)

Assured that the anti-theft module was the problem all along, the drive home was less stressful than the past few days. "Thank God the damn air conditioner still works," he said out loud. He turned down the volume on the truck radio as he thought about the situation. "A lot of things besides vehicles had encountered similar problems, in approximately in the same time frame. Cell phones and all kinds of electronic equipment going dead. And now this thing about botnets is all over the news. Huh!"

 Maybe it was nothing, but maybe what Major Morrisey had jokingly said earlier didn't seem so ridiculous. "What if...?" Ray thought to himself. "Just what if?" As he reached for his cell phone, his intelligence training kicked into high gear and hung up. "I'd better wait until I get inside to use a hard line. Anyone could be listening."

Ray pulled into the driveway and immediately headed for his computer. "Jack Walsh, Bell Labs. Here it is," Ray said to himself as he pulled up the telephone number from his database of contacts. "If anyone can find out what's going on, it's Jack." Leaning back on his chair he dialed the phone and called Jack, the head of the electrical engineering department at Bell Labs, an industrial research facility that handles highly sensitive contracts for the U.S. Defense Department, located in Murray Hills, New Jersey. Two rings later a voice on the other end answered in a disoriented tone of voice. "Hello?"

"Jack, this is Ray Darby. Sorry to bother you at this hour, but it's important."

"Who? It's 3:00 a.m.," responded Jack.

"Ray Darby," repeated Ray.

"Why are you calling at this time of the morning for? Are you ok?" questioned Jack.

"Yeah, I'm fine. I'm calling you from Taiwan," interjected Ray.

"I heard Bell Labs mentioned on the news the other morning. Something about uncovering a botnet scheme in Europe. Did your group have anything to do with it?" Ray asked.

"To an extent," responded Jack. "But I doubt that's why you're calling me at this time of the morning. What's up?"

"What do you know about anti-theft sensors installed in vehicles?" asked Ray.

"Woah. Slow down. I may be half awake, but give me a few minutes to put on some coffee and try to wake up. I can tell from your question that I'm going to be up for a while," said Jack, in a low, groggy tone of voice, as he maneuvered to get his body out of bed without waking his wife.

"Hold on a minute until I get downstairs. I don't want to wake Renee," replied Jack, making his way to the kitchen.

"Ok, anti-theft sensors in vehicles," Jack said, taking a dirty cup from the sink and rinsing it out.

"The correct term is transponder. Most vehicles are equipped with a transponder security system built into their ignition system. They're installed for security reasons and make it more difficult for car thieves to steal your vehicle," said Jack.

"Why all the interest in transponders? Don't tell me you've succumbed to trying to hotwire cars?" responded Jack, jokingly.

"No," interjected Ray, "But don't give me any ideas. How do they work and is it possible to electronically override it and shut a vehicle off from a remote location?"

"Hold on, I have to think about this for a few minutes," Jack said, pouring some reheated, day-old coffee into his cup and taking a sip. "Your car keys have transponder chips imbedded in them. Different car manufacturers use different types of chips in their keys. The transponders are made up of copper windings and a circuit board of some sort. When the proper key is put into the ignition, the induction coil in the column sends out an electromagnetic field. The filed energizes the transponder, which in turn sends a radio frequency signal back to the vehicle, allowing it to start."

"To answer the second part, anything is possible, Ray. Unless the transponder was defective, the system would have to be redesigned, or programmed somehow to shut down. Why all of a sudden this interest in transponders?" questioned Jack.

"I'm not sure," said Ray. "I'm just thinking out loud. But

if I sent you a transponder that has been intermittingly quitting, do you think you can check it out?"

"I suppose we could use some of the Labs diagnostics tools and try to run some random codes through it to see if anything unusual happens, but that could take some time. Let's not over simplify things. The transponder chip is only part of the equation. I'll need the onboard computer module that receives the radio frequency to start the vehicle and schematics of the circuits from the manufacturer. I'll probably end up destroying the one you give me in the process," said Jack. "How much time are you giving me to unravel this dilemma?"

"I'll have it on the next flight out of here as soon as I can get the mechanics at the motor pool to pull it out of the vehicle. You should have it within a few weeks. Oh, and try to find out where they're made and if any electronics used in U.S. security and military systems come from the same place. And check out any link to components used in cell phones. This information needs to be…"

"Hey, slow down. Remember, it's only 3:30 a.m. out here," interjected Jack, glancing at the wall clock. But Ray kept on talking, as if he hadn't heard a thing Jack said … "a high priority. Let me know what you find out."

"You don't want much do you? I'll see what I can do. But like I said, this will take some time and considerable effort. What do you want me to bill the time to, miscellaneous expenses?" questioned Jack, in his self-indulgent and dry sense of humor.

"I'll get the authorization and funding by the time you receive the parts. Talk to you soon and give my love to Renee," sated Ray, hanging up the phone.

Chapter 7: Programmed to Deceive

Several months had passed without a response from Jack, except to verify that he had received the transponder. After what seemed like forever, Ray received the call he was waiting for.

"Ray, this is Jack. Hey Ray, are you awake?" came the voice on the telephone.

"I am now," muffled Ray as he reached over to look at the alarm clock. "It's only 0330," responded Ray.

"Yeah, I know," stated Jack, laughing on the other end of the phone.

"How soon can you catch a flight to D.C?" asked Jack.

"As soon as I can catch a military fight out, possibly by the end of the week. Did you find out anything?" inquired Ray, in an overanxious voice.

"Can't talk now, I'm going back to bed," replied Jack. "But as long as you're up, I've gone ahead and made fight arrangements for you. You'd better get moving, your flight leaves at 0730. I'll pick you up at Andrews. Have a good flight."

"0730," said Ray, sitting on the edge of the bed with the receiver still clutched to his ear listening to the dial tone. "Right away," he said to himself.

"I expect a call when you get to D.C. to let me know where you're staying," Major Morrissey said, as she dropped Ray of at the hangar.

"From the tone of your voice, I believe you're going to miss me," responded Ray, giving her a quick kiss on the lips. Ray glanced back several times at Karen, as she sat watching him headed to the hangar, before leaving.

Exhausted from the flight and lack of sleep, Ray landed at Andrews Air Force Base outside of Washington, D.C. Jack was at the base to meet him.

"You must have found something, or you wouldn't have had me get out here so fast," said Ray, prompting Jack for answers.

"Wait until we're out of here," stated Jack, as they exited the hanger and walked across the parking lot to Jack's car.

"Where we headed?" Ray questioned, as they departed the base.

"First we're going to grab some breakfast and then get you set up in the hotel. We have a meeting at 01300 with Todd Keller, the Director of Homeland Security, and William Nipps, the Secretary of Defense," responded Jack, in a direct tone of voice.

"You do realize what you've uncovered, don't you? The shit's going to really hit the fan now. Grab the backpack from behind your seat, open it up, and pull out the folder," Jack said, pointing to the pink backpack on the floor behind his seat.

"You mean the one with Barbie on the front?" asked Ray. "You've got to be kidding me." Ray opened the briefcase and pulled out the folder with 'Barbie's Summer Collection' scribbled across the cover in black marker.

"What the heck is this stuff?" asked Ray, in a look of bewilderment, as he started flipping through the pages.

"That's my daughter's backpack. I use it so anyone looking at it doesn't see beyond what they think it is," said Jack

"So this is what Engineers at Bell Labs do? It really tells me a lot about your clandestine job with the Government," said Ray, laughing as he thumbed through the pages. "But don't worry, your secret is safe with me."

"That's it there," said Jack. "Pull it out and read it." Ray anxiously read each line, flipping back and forth between the spreadsheets, and on occasion, pictures of Barbie's outfits. The spreadsheets listed electronic components, their manufacturer, and country of origin, ranging from cell phone to military and computer hardware.

"What the hell?" stated Ray, in a puzzled, but confident voice. "I had a gut feeling, but I was only speculating," he said, staring in Jack's direction as he sat back in the seat. "You're right, I think the shit is going to hit the fan."

"Who all knows about this?" Ray inquired.

"I've already briefed the Director of Homeland Security and the Secretary of Defense," said Jack. "We've been asked to attend a briefing to the President and Congressional Subcommittee of the situation."

"No," said Ray. "I mean the thing you have for Barbie?"

Jack turned up the volume on the car radio to catch the morning's headline news at the top of the hour as they pulled into the entrance to the underground parking lot.

"In today's news, increasing gas prices hit an all time high of $5.40 per gallon at the pumps. This is a 22-cent rise within the last ten days. The increase is a result of the continued increase in energy consumption by emerging industrialized nations, namely China and India. In other news....."

"I get tired of listening to the same thing every day. Over, and over again," Jack muttered in disgust, turning off the radio. "Nothing ever changes. It's just politics as usual."

Jack and Ray arrived at the office of the Director for Homeland Security. After signing in, and passing through security, they were issued visitor passes and escorted to the meeting room.

"Well get started in just a few minutes," came a voice from the front of the room. It was the Director for Homeland Security, Todd Keller. "We're just waiting for the President to arrive. Please have a seat....."

Ray was about to sit next to Jack when he glanced up to notice the President arrive, flanked by the Secretary of Defense, the Chief of the Arms Services Committee, and Ambassador to the UN. Ray leaned against Jack and clutched his arm. "The President just arrived."

"Mr. President," stated Keller, looking directly at him. "Just let me know when you're ready and we will get started."

"In just a few minutes," responded the President, shaking hands and engaging in cordial conversation with members of Congress.

Chapter 8: I've Got A Secret

"Before we begin, I would like to take the opportunity to introduce the two gentlemen seated at the back of the room - Jack Walsh from Bell Labs, and Major Ray Darby," stated the Secretary of Defense. "As most of you may know, Jack oversees the electrical engineering research department at Bell Labs. Jack and his team at Bell Labs are credited for the detection and breakup of the European botnet scheme we've all been hearing about lately. Major Darby is with naval intelligence and stationed at Ching Chuan Kang Air Force Base in Taiwan. Major Darby is here today because he provided insight into the communications and electrical disruptions, which is the focus of this briefing. Thank you for all attending. Let's get started. I'll turn the remainder of the briefing over to the Director of Homeland Security, Todd Keller."

"In front of you is a copy of the report outlining the current issues," stated Keller. "You have been sent copies of the report prior to this meeting, and I trust you have all had a chance to read and become familiar with its contents. I must remind everyone that the information outlined in the report is classified information relevant to the security of the United States."

With that opening statement, Keller laid out all of the facts-point by point. "We are faced with a paradigm. While we remain the greatest nation in the world today, both economically and militarily, we no longer manufacture the basic commodities we use. It's not cost effective. The majority of the electronic components that go into products we use every day and take for granted are not manufactured here, or by one of our strategic allies. Weapons for the defense of the United States are not even manufactured here. Our technology is exported to other emerging countries such as China, India, Pakistan, Taiwan, South Korea, Vietnam, and Mexico to be manufactured. It falls under the umbrella of the Free Trade Agreement. It started with Mexico and Canada, then spread to the Asian triangle. Soon it will include Central and South America. We are no longer the ruler of our fate. Here are the facts as we know them at this point.

Fact No. 1: Over the last year there had been a frequency of power failures; not only in the U.S., but also in Canada, Europe, the Middle East, Australia, and Japan, to name a few of the major countries. The usual circumstances - vehicles stalling, cell phones going dead, televisions blacking out. The frequency of these occurrences was low at first, but they have been gradually becoming more prevalent. We have recently been monitoring problems with our military vehicles, and aircraft not functioning. They intermittently shut off for no apparent reason and then start up again.

Fact No. 2: Intelligence services have been recently monitoring the increase in sales of petroleum on the world market to China. The frequency and volume of their imports have been steadily increasing and has almost doubled within the last eight months. We don't believe this is strictly tied to their industrial growth.

Fact No. 3: China has launched two satellites within the last four months. We know that they were joint ventures with their strategic trading partners, Iran and North Korea, but until now we could only speculate what their purpose was.

Fact No. 4: Right now, there are at least 5 major terrorist nations in the world, all unfriendly towards U.S. interests - China, Iran, North Korea, Syria, and Russia. They all have one thing in common, well two: China and Russia. But China is the main thread of commonality providing the other nations with the technology and materials to sponsor terrorist activities around the world, and against the U.S. interests and our allies.

Fact No. 5: As stated earlier, just about everything made today is made in China. Everything from toasters, cell phones, microchips, to components installed in our stealth bombers, nuclear submarines, and nuclear missile guidance systems. Even the Hubble telescope and components used in our missile defense system. Everything has some type of electronic component made in China.

As we are reminded by the heads of our leading companies and by members of Congress, there is nothing wrong with having products manufactured elsewhere at a cheaper cost. That allows U.S. companies to maintain high profit margins, invest in R&D, and spur growth," continued Keller.

"We must not forget the multi-million dollars in bonuses and incentive packages corporations paid their CEO's last year based on their profits," interjected the President.

After the round of low level laughter subsided, Keller continued. "We are living in a new world where Global Trading and eliminating trade barriers is not only the norm, but it is what's required. At the end of the day, we are still getting what we would have designed and the product we expect. Or are we?"

"While stationed in Taiwan, Major Darby became aware of a sequence of fragmented and unnatural occurrences that were developing. He wasn't able to put the pieces together until he contacted Jack Walsh to see if it was possible to discern if the 'what should be' equates to 'what is'."

"Over the past three months, Jack and the staff at Bell Labs, were able to identify a reoccurring anomaly within several electrical devices he was testing. With assistance from the U.S. military, selected electronic and computer chip manufacturers, communications companies, computer software developers, and selected manufacturers, a pattern of deception was uncovered, that left unchallenged, will leave the United States militarily impotent to the point where we cannot defend ourselves or our allies."

Keller continued, stopping only to take a brief drink from the glass of water on the table. "What was discovered were irregularities in the electronic components installed in just about everything. On the surface, everything works perfectly as designed. But after reviewing the microprocessors and circuit boards in these devices, there is a clear difference between what was designed and what was manufactured. The differences are subtle and have gone without notice. But nevertheless, they are there."

"For instance, look at the random failure of the transponder Major Darby had sent to Bell Labs. After analysis, using state-of-the-art electronic equipment to jam communications, Bell Labs was able to pin-point an irregularity on the circuit board that created the disruption. Working with the designer of the board, it was clear there was a discrepancy between the design and the manufactured circuit. A microchip was added that was not part of the original design and the circuit board was deliberately altered in the manufacturing process. Once this was discovered and we were able to control when the circuit was either on or off, we knew we were on to something. The schematics for a number of high value devices used for defense purposes including armor vehicles, missile guidance systems, fighter aircraft electrical systems, nuclear warhead components, and the new missile defense system were reviewed. The list goes on as outlined in the report, but I doubt if we have scratched the surface. All of these components have one source of manufacture – China."

Keller paused, took another short sip of water, then continued. "Now we have identified the cause. But what triggers the disruptions? If you note in the report, we have gone back and created a spreadsheet of the dates of reported incidences ranging from cell phone disruptions to communications and transportation disruptions that we know about. We also tracked the trajectory of any known satellites or aircraft overhead. In everyone of these occurrences, we have identified the disruption due to satellite interference. In particular, the satellites launched by China, which to this day, they refuse to identify their purpose other than their standard 'catch phrases' for media attention. Now we know their purpose. It is clear beyond all reasonable doubt what their motive is. What is unclear is the timeframe for full implementation of their plan to disrupt and shut down our military defenses."

Chapter 9: Menu Options

"If what you have outlined in the report is true, and I don't doubt you for a second, it is a clear act of aggression against the United States and our national interests. It requires an immediate response," stated the President. "Do you have any reason to believe, at this point, the Chinese suspect we are onto them?"

"No Sir," responded Keller. "We believe the testing performed to date has been done without disclosing or doing anything that would lead China to suspect we are aware of their intentions."

"Two questions. Number one, do we have a timetable for securing our military defenses; namely the anti-missile defenses and nuclear warheads; and number two, what options are available to respond in the event we cannot bring our defenses on line in time?" asked the Chief of the Armed Services.

"As presented in the report, there is a schedule of necessary and immediate actions we must take to thwart their intentions. But we must move quickly and pray to God that we are not too late to counter this aggression before we are attacked," responded Keller.

"What about forcing a resolution at the U.N. Security Council, calling for a vote of condemnation against the Chinese, and requiring they immediately destroy the satellites?" questioned the U.S. Ambassador to the U.N.

"At the offset, I need to be clear that going to the U.N. is not our first option, or in our interest at this time," stated Keller.

"I agree," stated the President. "Once the cat is out of the bag, there is no telling how the Chinese and their terrorist thugs will respond. With United States and allied troops in harm's way in the Middle East, South Korea, Japan, and Taiwan, we must be decisive and quick to respond."

"Getting back to the main point of urgency, what options do we have?" inquired the Secretary of Defense.

"As outlined in the report, a five step approach has been developed as follows," stated Keller.

> "Step 1: We have identified and ranked strategic defense weapons in order of their effectiveness to counter an immediate attack. We are in the process of replacing the affected circuit boards where we can with ones now being manufactured here. Where this is not an option or where time is the critical issue we are attempting to perform what I term bypass surgery, by re-circuiting around the infected area and cutting off the direct route to the microchip. As you can see from the timeline, we feel we can have these weapons in place and secure within 6-8 months. Our first priority is up-fitting our missile defense system and nuclear warheads, both land-based and sub-based.

We are also in the process of up-fitting the weapons in use by our ground forces.

Step 2: While time is on our side, we will continue engaging the Chinese in diplomatic talks to pressure them to state the purpose of the two satellites. At the same time, our Press Secretary will engage the media in a propaganda campaign identifying the power shortages and disruptions on outdated equipment and infrastructure.

Step 3: We haven't fully tested our missile defense capabilities and we don't know what the odds are, if any, of taking out a satellite in orbit. With the assistance of NASA, there are several satellites in orbit, but there is one in particular that is scheduled to enter the earth's atmosphere sometime within the next month and burn up on re-entry. We propose to use this satellite to test our missile defense system. If we're successful at destroying it, we will have the advantage when it comes to dealing with the Chinese in the Security Council.

Step 4: When the first two parts are in place, the U.S. is to request a special session of the U.N. Security Council to expose what is going on and demand the immediate destruction of the satellites under U.N. supervision. With the false media coverage in place, we believe they will assume we are still vulnerable and they have time for continued debate and prepare a response in the Security Council.

Parallel to this, we will prepare a routine mission for the space shuttle to the international space station. In the event we are unsuccessful in taking out the satellites with our missiles, this will put us in a first strike position to intercept and destroy their satellites from space.

Step 5: And as a last resort, if they refuse, we will have no choice but to destroy the satellites and launch an immediate nuclear strike against them. If we can catch them off guard, we can hit them hard before they can have a chance to retaliate in full force. And by that time we will be able to increase both our ground forces and have our nuclear subs in position."

"The hell with the U.N," responded the President. "Let me know when and I'll order the Navy to take out the satellites. We will then engage them in diplomatic discussions at the U.N., and it will be on our terms and timetable, not theirs. They're not going to retaliate. Once we take out the satellites, it will be obvious that we were onto them. They won't do a damn thing except twist the facts and spout their condemnation of us to the U.N. Security Council and media, as usual."

"Ok, hold on a second!" exclaimed the Treasury Secretary, thumping the eraser end of his pencil against the table. "Before everyone gets gung-ho on solving this situation militarily, we'd better take a hard look at the economic repercussions. The current situation is that our housing market is in the worst slump in 30-years and investment banking is on the verge of collapse. We've had to bail out Wall Street brokerage firms within the last six months, gas prices are at an all time high, as well as unemployment, and shakeups in the auto and airline industries are teetering on bankruptcy. It's anyone's guess what's going to happen tomorrow. How long we can sustain our military troop deployments around the globe at it present cost is also questionable."

"It's time we face reality. The fact is, the Chinese government has underwritten us to the tune of around $6-trillion dollars. Piss of China and they could flood the world market with U.S. dollars, driving down the value of the dollar, and throwing this country into a crisis I can't even contemplate," continued the Treasury Secretary.

"If they do that, they're not only going to take us down, but also the rest of the major industrial nations along with us, including themselves. I don't believe they would do that. They would have nothing to gain with the total collapse of the world financial market," stated the President, in a strong, positive voice.

"Are you sure about that Mr. President?" responded the Treasury Secretary, in a confrontational tone. "The minute we take out their satellites, there's more than one way to retaliate besides militarily."

"I am more than aware of our debt to China. I'm not disputing the other side of the coin you've laid out. We can't base our action on what we speculate they might do, especially considering the grave consequences that confront us if we do nothing less than a military option," replied the President.

The President, with the utmost urgency, directed the Secretary of Defense to oversee the status and replacement of the altered parts in both offensive and defensive military weapons. He also directed the 'Task Force' to meet with him on a weekly basis to brief him on the progress of the modifications, and any changes that develop.

Chapter 10: 007

Ray spent the following several days visiting friends in Alexandria, VA., taking in the hot spots, and relaxing.

Ray met with Jack and his wife Renee for a light dinner and drinks to catch up on both old and new times. Renee hadn't seen Ray for nearly six months and the dinner conversation was focused on his love life.

"So, when are you going to get married and settle down?" inquired Renee.

"At the rate he's going, it won't be until he's in his late 40's," interjected Jack.

"Now you be quiet," Renee said, looking at Jack sternly. "Anyway, Jack told me you were going with someone. It's about time you found someone to be with. Tell me all about her. Is it serious? Is she military?" prodded Renee.

"She's a nurse temporarily stationed at the naval base in Taiwan," said Ray.

"What's her name?" inquired Renee.

"Major Morrissey," responded Ray.

"Ray, you know what I mean. What's her name?" Renee repeated.

"Her name is Karen," responded Ray.

"Now, that wasn't so hard, was it?" questioned Renee.

"Ok, enough with the interrogation," interjected Jack. "Let Ray enjoy the evening. He will get married when he's ready."

"Ok, I'll change the subject," responded Renee. "But at the rate he's going, it won't be in his forties, it will be more like his fifties."

Ray was dropped of at the Wyndham hotel, ready to call it a night and leave the jet lag and stress from the previous days behind. Ray opened a beer that was in the cooler in his room, flipped on the TV for background noise, and hit a hot shower.

"Ah, boy did that feel good," Ray said as he dried off and laid out on the bed. "I think I'll sleep until noon. Let's see what's on the television," he said, surfing the stations to try to find something interesting to watch. "Great choices - television, current movies, or the usual sleazy adult porn. So much for television," Ray thought to himself, as he hit the off button, closed his eyes, and thought about Karen.

The sound of the phone ringing awakened Ray. "7:30 a.m., so much for sleeping until noon," he said, rolling over and picking up the receiver. "Hello?"

"Bond, James Bond?" was the reply on the other end in a flirtatious, but childish English accent.

"Karen?" Ray asked. "Is that you? What's going on in Taiwan?"

"I don't know. I'm not in Taiwan," responded Karen.

"What? Where are you?" asked Ray.

"I'm downstairs in the hotel lobby. Did you miss me?" questioned Karen.

"If I didn't know better, I'd think you' were following me," said Ray.

"Well, are you going to invite me up or do you want me to just stand down here?" questioned Karen.

"As long as you're down there, would you mind grabbing a bagel and cup of black coffee from the restaurant?" asked Ray. "Oh, and have them toast the bagel dark. Nothing on it."

Ray opened the room door after several kicks from Karen's foot, to see her clutching a paper bag and two large styrofoam cups in her hands.

"Room Service-coffee and a bagel," Karen said, standing in the doorway with a pleasant smile. Ray took them from her and popped the plastic lid on the cup only to see a light brown substance instead of the black coffee he was waiting for.

"What is this stuff?" inquired Ray.

"Wrong cup," returned Karen, as she took it from Ray. "It's one-half coffee, and one-half hot chocolate. This is your cup," she said, handing it to him. "Would you like to try it?"

"No thanks," responded Ray. "I like my coffee black, although yours does smell good."

"Well, once you've tried half and half, you'll never go back to just black coffee," replied Karen, laughing.

"You're bad," responded Ray, also laughing at Karen's lame sense of humor.

Karen looked great standing next to him in her running shoes, tan shorts and Cirque de' Sole tee shirt. Her mousey-blond hair, sparkling blue eyes and attractive features had Ray questioning why he hadn't made a serious pass at her. He had liked her from the first time they met and she had been in his thoughts a lot recently. They got along great. "Maybe it's time I settled down," he thought.

Ray walked over to Karen and put his arms around her waist and held her close.

Yeah," said Ray, in a lonely tone.

"Yeah, what?" responded Karen, turning and looking directly into his eyes.

"Yeah, I missed you," replied Ray, running his hand up the back of her neck and kissing her. The kiss was short and tender, but made the point. Karen put her arms around him in a gesture of affection and they kissed, this time longer and more passionate.

"How long you here for?" asked Ray, still holding her.

"Five days - until next Sunday," responded Karen. "I've been reassigned to the Pentagon for the duration of my enlistment at the end of May."

"Damn it! When did this happen?" questioned Ray in a frustrated tone.

"Right after you left. I wasn't sure when you were returning to Taiwan, and I wanted to see you again," replied Karen, looking up into Ray's eyes.

"Any plans for the next few days?" asked Ray.

"Not really. Maybe just hang out together and do some sightseeing. Why?" asked Karen.

"I promised my parents I would drive up to Danbury, Connecticut to see them for a few days. I would like you to go with me," said Ray, whispering in her ear and holding her close.

"I'd like that," responded Karen. "But I hope you're not driving a Ford. My God, we would never get there."

"Let's get out on the street and get some fresh air. I'll race you to the elevator," Ray said, grabbing his coffee and bagel and heading out the door, leaving Karen scrambling to catch up.

"You are such a JERK!" she yelled out, laughing as she shut the door and walked down the corridor, not even trying to catch up.

The ride down the elevator was too short to plan their morning. "What did you want to do?" asked Ray.

"I'm not sure. This is my first time to D.C. There's so much to see and do, but I suppose you have already been everywhere?" she questioned.

"Not really. I've been busy visiting friends and I haven't had a chance to enjoy everything," responded Ray, even though he had been to D.C. before. Ray wanted to do it all over again, this time, one-on-one with Karen.

"Let's start at the Capitol Building and then decide where to go from there," stated Ray, holding Karen's hand and hailing a cab.

"Maybe we can go to the Central Park," said Karen in a teasing voice.

"That's in lower Manhattan, not D.C.," responded Ray, shaking his head. "You are such an airhead."

"I know that," responded Karen.

"You know you're an airhead?" questioned Ray, sliding close to her as they entered the cab.

"Not that part," responded Karen. "But when we go through New York, I want to stop at the site of 911 too."

The morning went by fast. They didn't spend much time going down the historic route. Instead, Ray found himself in women's fashion stores while Karen tried on clothes, shoes, and more shoes.

"Honey, you're confusing me. I thought you wanted to see History, not shop all day?" inquired Ray.

"If I'm going to meet your parents, I have to have something to wear. Did you just call me Honey?" she responded, exiting the dressing room and looking at Ray with a romantic smile.

By mid afternoon, Ray and Karen stopped to eat, have a few drinks, and relax before checking out of their hotels and picking up the rental car to drive to

Danbury. It was later than Ray had planned on leaving, but they were finally off to meet his parents.

Chapter 11: Morning Showers

Not having completely missed the end of the day rush-hour traffic out of the D.C. and Baltimore areas, the drive up the Garden State Parkway was tiring. Ray knew he could drive straight through to Danbury, but it was late and Karen had already snuggled up to him and had fallen asleep on his shoulder. Ray decided to call it a night and find a hotel. He pulled into a hotel parking lot and turned off the car, and sat quietly, listening to the latest news on the radio.

"This just in from AFP Global News Agency: Earlier today, Defense Secretary William Nipps held a news conference where he briefed the news media. He said at 3:20 this afternoon, he ordered the U.S.S. Lake Erie, located near Hawaii and armed with an SM-3 missile designed to knock down incoming missiles, to intercept and destroy a disabled communications satellite that was headed for earth. At 4:00, the Joint Space Operations' Center at Vandenburgh confirmed the breakup of the satellite. The objective was to intercept the satellite, reduce the mass that might survive reentry and vector that mass as best as possible to unpopulated areas, ideally the ocean. Defense Secretary Nipps said the shoot down was approved by the President and that the satellite strike was a one-time incident. However, this is seen by some as a blurring the lines between defending against a hostile long-range missile and targeting satellites in orbit. This elaborate intercept has already triggered worries from some international leaders, who could see it as a thinly disguised attempt to test an

anti-satellite weapon – one that could take out another nation's orbiting communications and spy spacecraft. Within hours of the reported success, China said it condemned the action taken by the United States and sees it as a hostile act that could have intense international ramifications, but stopped short of requesting a meeting of the U.N. Security Council."

"Where are we?" asked Karen, raising her head off of Ray's shoulder and opening her eyes to look around.

"We're at a Marriott Hotel just outside of Newark, New Jersey. It's late and I think we're both overly exhausted from shopping to try to drive straight through. We can stay here tonight," said Ray.

"Sounds great. You get the bags and I'll check us in," she said, getting out of the car and stretching.

"What room am I in?" inquired Ray, as they got on the hotel elevator.

"407," answered Karen.

"What room are you in? asked Ray.

"407," replied Karen. "We're sharing the room. Do you think you can handle it?" she taunted, in a sleepy voice, resting her head on his arm.

Ray opened the hotel room door and put the luggage on the dresser next to the bed. "Single bed?" Ray muttered, glancing over at Karen.

"I didn't want to be alone," she said. Ray and Karen skipped the formality of unpacking. They both kicked off their shoes, and before Ray could pull the bed covers down Karen jumped on the bed and pulled Ray down next to her. Ray moved his hands over her as they passionately held each other and kissed.

"Honey, no sex until we're married, ok? I mean, unless you don't want to get married." she said, softly running her fingers along his waist and tickling him.

"No!" said Ray, laughing.

"No, you don't want to get married, or no, you're ticklish?" prodded Karen.

Ray stopped short, and in a serious look, kissed her softly on the lips. "I hope you're not one of those women who want a big engagement ring and wedding," he said.

"No, just a big engagement ring," said Karen as she kissed Ray, laid her head against his, and fell asleep.

Ray opened his eyes the next morning to see Karen already awake, her head sharing the pillow and gazing at his face.

"Good morning," she said in a soft voice, pushing her body closer beside him under the covers and then on top. Ray put his arms around her, running his hand up her back and under her hair.

"Good morning," was his response as they kissed.

"Come on, we've got to get going if we're ever going to be get to your parents. I've got dubs on the shower first," she shouted, looking at the time on the phone clock and jumping off the bed.

"Or we could shower together," responded Ray.

"Not until we're married," said Karen, putting her hand on his chest and pushing him back. "You'll just have to wait."

"Then save me some hot water," he said, as Karen shut the bathroom door behind her.

They had the complimentary hotel breakfast before Karen checked out and Ray loaded the luggage in the car. Except for the short stop to fuel up and find a Dunkin' Donuts so Karen could have her usual cup of hot chocolate and coffee mix, they headed into Manhattan to walk through Central Park, then to the 911 site to reflect on what had happened, and to pay their respects to those who lost their lives.

Once they cleared the rush hour traffic snarl leading out of Manhattan from all directions, the remainder of the drive was less stressful. Karen rolled the windows down to catch the warm breeze on her face and ran through the local FM stations on the radio until she found some music.

"Great! Frank Sinatra," said Karen as she sat close to Ray. "Are you going to call your parents and let them know when we will be arriving? And are you going to tell them we're engaged."

"I was going to surprise them, but you're probably right," said Ray, reaching for his cell phone to call his parents. Ray left a brief message on their answering machine, only mentioning he would be arriving late afternoon. He avoided saying anything about being engaged, or letting on Karen was with him. He wanted it to be a surprise.

Chapter 12: Meet the Parents

As Ray pulled into the driveway of the farmhouse, he saw his mother peering through the front picture window with excited anticipation on his arrival. No sooner had Ray turned off the motor when his mother and father were at the car to greet him.

"Ray! You lost some weight," was Edna's greeting, giving him a mother's hug and kiss on the cheek. At the same time, Ray was trying to reach around her to shake his father's hand.

"Pop the trunk and I'll help you with the luggage," Frank insisted, while starting to walk to the rear of the car. Karen stood leaning over the car top, watching the focused attention on Ray from his parents. While still hugging Ray, Edna caught Karen's movement as she turned to shut the car door.

"Ray? You didn't tell me Karen was with you? What a wonderful surprise," she said as she released Ray. "And she is every bit as lovely as you said," continued Edna, moving around the car to give Karen a hug and kiss.

"How did you know who I am?" responded Karen, smiling and bending over to return the hug. At that point, Ray was waving his hands frantically and making gestures to get his mother's attention in an attempt to say "DON'T GO THERE!"

"Ray told us all about you whenever he called. You're exactly as he described you. I think the only reason he called so often was just to talk about you. And it's about time he came for a visit and brought an attractive woman with him," Edna said in a firm and positive tone, looking over at Ray.

"Yeah," interjected Ray's father, pulling the luggage out of the trunk. "He could have brought a guy home instead."

"Is Jim home, dad?" asked Ray.

"Your brother is out in Las Vegas with some friends for a week. There's some electronics convention he wanted to go to. At least that's the excuse he used," responded Frank.

"Let Ray and his father get the luggage. I'm sure they have a lot to talk about. Come in and I'll make some coffee and we can get acquainted," said Edna, gesturing her towards the front door.

"Ray, you coming too?" asked Karen, looking for support, with a puppy love tone to her voice.

"I'll be right in," responded Ray. "Mom? Do you have any hot chocolate?" yelled Ray, as the front screen door closed.

Ray met his father in the front hallway as he was coming down the stairs. "I put your luggage in your bedroom and Karen's in the guest room."

"What do you think, Dad?" Ray asked.

"About what?" responded Frank.

"You know, Karen," responded Ray.

"I like her. You go and sit with the women and I'll grab a couple of cups of coffee and be right in to get acquainted. No telling what types of questions your mother is stirring up," stated Frank in a overly loud voice.

"Oh, you be quiet. Karen and I have just been sitting here, having a lovely conversation and getting to know each other," returned Edna. "Frank, Karen said her parents live in upstate New York, Vernon. It's about a half-hour east of Syracuse."

"Honey, come and sit beside me," Karen said, gesturing to Ray.

"Honey?" Frank said to himself with lip gestures, as he looked at Edna.

As Ray sat down, Karen scooched up to him. "When are you going to tell your parents we're engaged?" she softly whispered in Ray's ear.

"In just a bit," Ray whispered.

"Do you want me to tell them?" she responded back.

"In a minute," replied Ray, as he started to take a sip of coffee.

"Honey, don't you have something important you want tell our father and mother?" she blurted out. Ray was caught off guard and sprayed coffee over himself as he recovered from chocking. As he began to blot up the coffee, he looked over at Karen. "Did anyone ever tell you you're annoying?" he replied, in a soft and teasing voice.

"Just once," responded Karen, smiling and holding his hand. "Sorry."

"Is there something you want to tell us?" asked Edna, as both her and Frank looked at Ray.

"I guess now is as good a time as any," Ray said, putting his arm around Karen. "Besides coming home to see you, I wanted you to meet Karen and let you know that I have asked her to marry me."

"Excuse me? Did I hear you right? Did you say you're engaged?" responded Frank, sitting down across from them. "How old are you now Ray, mid fifties?" prodded Frank.

"You're in your fifties?" responded Karen with a startled look.

"No. I'm not in my fifties. I'm only thirty-six," stated Ray.

"Well, you certainly are not," interjected Edna. "It hasn't even been a year since you sat right there and swore you weren't planning on *ever* getting married until you were in your fifties," said Edna in a stern tone of voice, glancing at Karen and trying to hold back her laughter.

Then something Karen had never thought about just came out. "You're not gay, are you?" she asked, in an excited voice, as an expression of fear came over her.

"What? No, I'm not gay!" exclaimed Ray, looking with disbelief that she even asked that question.

"When I saw Karen, I knew it was serious," stated Frank.

"Ray, I just don't know what you're thinking," stated Edna, in a scolding tone and shaking her head.

"What are you talking about?" asked Ray, looking at his mother in bewilderment.

"I would expect before you proposed to Karen, you would have bought her an engagement ring," she said.

Ray started to defend himself, but before he could get anything out his mother interjected. "Now you two have tomorrow to go downtown or to the Mall. You buy Karen an engagement ring and don't you even think of coming home without one. You can charge it on your father's credit card," directed Edna.

Ray and Karen spent the early afternoon going back and forth between several of the well known jewelry stores in town and Danbury Fair Mall, comparing prices and learning everything about diamond rings. It didn't take Karen long to make a decision. She knew exactly what she wanted. She just had to keep telling Ray that she was only kidding when she said she wanted a big ring.

"Honey, the size isn't important. I just want something small and plain, one we pick out together," she said.

"Ok, Ok. You win. You can have a small diamond if that's what you want, but it has to be perfect," said Ray, with the emphasis on perfect.

That settled, Karen selected a 1/2 karat of impeccable clarity and a plain gold band with both their names and date engraved on the inside.

"I like that on you," Ray said, putting his arm around her and giving her a kiss.

"I do too," stated Karen, looking at Ray.

"I agree. You made an excellent selection on the ring," said the jeweler, closing the display case and making his way to the counter to make out the receipt.

"Any chance we could pick up the ring later today?" asked Ray as he handed the jeweler the credit card.

"Well, we're not too busy this afternoon, so I think I can have it ready, say, in about three hours. Stop back around 5:00," stated the jeweler, giving Karen a wink.

"Ray and Karen killed time strolling through the mall hand-in-hand, popping in and out of women's clothing stores, with a quick stop at a record store to buy a Sinatra CD. They ended their mall excretion at Hooters for a few drinks, a bite to eat, and some visual enticement for Ray, contrary to his objections, before returning to the jewelry store.

With the ring firmly on her finger, Karen was teary-eyed as they pulled into the driveway. Ray turned off the engine and they sat quietly listening to the soft tapping of rain hitting the car roof and windshield and

Sinatra in the CD player. It was a romantic moment and Karen snuggled close to Ray in the front seat listening to their favorite song, *Summer Wind*.

"Thanks for the ring," she said, laying her head against his arm.

"Just don't lose it," Ray responded, as he tenderly kissed her on her forehead and pulled her closer.

"So, when are we getting married? I was thinking on my birthday, June 17th," said Karen in a low whisper looking up at Ray.

The three days at his parents flew by too fast. Karen and Edna were like grade school girl friends, always together, and inseparable. For the first time, being home meant more to Ray than the usual, and often too short, a visit. His parents seemed to have renewed energy with Karen there. It was a time for relaxing. It also meant being part of Ray's family for Karen. Thoughts of returning to Taiwan and the potential conflicts that lie ahead had been the furthest from his mind.

Chapter 13: Chinese Takeout

Ray flew back to Taiwan at taxpayer's expense on a military C-138 cargo plane, stopping off at Hawaii and Guam before landing at the airbase in Taipei. The long trip was boring, except for the brief conversations with other military personnel and thinking of what Karen was doing. As the airbase landing strip came into view, Ray knew he had to focus on returning to duty and the situation at hand.

The first few days dragged on endlessly without Karen. Then as the weeks went by and the pace picked up, everything was back to normal, except for the erratic power and communication blackouts. Ray's truck continued to stall intermittently along with other military vehicles, but not as frequently as in the past.

Ray and Karen kept in daily contact through e-mail and by telephone at least once a week. Ray and Jack still kept in touch, but on an infrequent basis. Jack was out of the loop on updated intelligence information and on what was going on behind the scenes, or so he said. He had opted to take an early retirement from Bell Labs after it was acquired by Alcatel-Lucent Technologies, a multinational French company that provides hardware, software, and services to telecommunication service providers.

Ray had been back for only a short time when the base was put on an elevated threat level. Exhausted from an extended shift, Ray had left for the drive home when his beeper went off and he was ordered back to the base. "Damn it," Ray said as he hit the brakes and spun the truck around on a dime like the NASCAR drivers, but not as smooth. "Cool. It needs some work, but cool," he thought to himself.

"What's going on?" he inquired, noticing the threat level had been raised to severe as he passed through the security mantraps and entered the SCIF for lockdown. All eyes were fixed to the television monitors in the briefing room and people were scrambling as intelligence from every military sector was streaming in.

"We have late breaking news, just in. CNN has just been advised that the President is to address the nation momentarily. While we are waiting, Rachel Dove is standing by at the United Nations in New York. Rachel, what can you tell us about what's happening?" asked the CNN commentator.

"What I do know is that the U.S. military has been placed on high alert and that the Chinese Ambassador to the United Nations was summoned to the White House this morning around 2:30 a.m. One moment, I have just been handed something. Ok. I have just been informed that the U.N. Security Council had been called into emergency session shortly after 5:00 a.m. this morning and has been in chambers since that time. What I have...." stated Rachel.

"Rachel, sorry to have to cut you off, but we have been informed that the President is entering the Capitol rotunda and is about to speak," interrupted the CNN commentator.

"Good Evening. Over the past seven months, the United States, along with Canada, and our strategic European and Asian allies, have experienced an ongoing series of interruptions to our power grids, communications, and transportation services. The continued interruptions have not only affected our daily lives, but are a national security threat. To that end, five months ago I set up a joint commission, chaired by Senator Paul Smith of the Energy Commission, Todd Keller, the Director for Homeland Security, and top executives from the nation's leading energy and communications' service suppliers. Their mission was to identify the causes for these interruptions, fix them, and make recommendations to alleviate future occurrences.

Over the past three decades, the United States and our trading partners have been engaged in trade agreements that have benefited our economies and have brought underdeveloped nations to the forefront in technology and manufacturing. While the United States has been, and remains at the forefront of cutting edge engineering and design, the majority of our high-tech society relies on these products being manufactured by our trading partners, mainly India, South Korea, Japan, and China. These products include everyday commodities such as televisions and cell-phones, as well as electronic components in our cars, and airlines. Many of the components vital to our missile guidance systems, including our aircraft and submarines, are manufactured in foreign countries as well. At a higher threat level, the electronics in our military defenses were also prone to failure, leaving the United States and our allied vulnerable to attack. In particular, our military bases in the Middle East, South Korea, Taiwan, and Japan.

Last January, China launched a satellite, and within three months of that launch, a second satellite was launched. Both launches were unannounced, and when questioned as to their purpose, the world was told they were weather satellites. Since their launch, the United States has been closely monitoring them.

With the assistance from Bell Laboratories, we were able to isolate and identify the cause for many of the interruptions. The power blackouts, communications and transportation disruptions are the direct result of interference from the two satellites launched by China.

What we have uncovered are changes to the design of the electronic components. The changes were not random. They were a deliberate modification to the manufacturing process in such as way that when an electric signal was transmitted from the satellites, the electronic device would stop working, power grids would shut down, and communication would be disrupted. Thanks to our intelligence agency, we were able to identify the threat posed early on. This gave the United States time to work with our strategic allies to identify vital military components affected, and to redesign and replace them with new components. For the past two months, I ordered the United States military be placed on a heightened threat level. On Wednesday, I briefed the Joint Chiefs' of Staff and Congress on the situation. Yesterday morning I ordered the threat level to be raised to severe. At this time, we are ready to meet any challenges posed by China, if the need arises. At the same time, I summoned the Chinese Ambassador to the White House to discuss the grave situation. I informed him that in no uncertain terms, the United States is prepared to launch an immediate military strike, including the use of nuclear weapons, against China if any hostile action towards the United States or any of our allies is detected. I have asked our Ambassador to the United Nations to request an emergency meeting of the Security Council to present the information supporting our position, and calling for a vote to condemn China and the immediate destruction of their satellites. The United States and its allied have urged the Chinese for an immediate response which has gone unanswered. At 2:00 a.m. this morning, the Pentagon informed me that satellite surveillance showed a military buildup by Chinese troops, ships, and aircraft in the China Sea. This buildup of military troops and equipment is within quick striking reach of South Korea, Taiwan and Japan. This action by the Chinese is a direct threat to the security of the United States and a provocation for war. Therefore, I ordered our military to destroy the two satellites. At 2:15 a.m. this morning, the United States launched two surface to air missiles from undisclosed bases. At 2:27 a.m. I was informed that the missiles hit their targets and were successful in destroying the satellites. At the same time, I called China's leader and reaffirmed the United States' position and called for the immediate pull-back of their military forces in the region. I informed the Chinese government that any hostile action towards the United States, or our allies in the region, as a result of the destruction of the satellites, will be countered militarily, including the use of nuclear weapons. The United States will not be held hostage by any country, nor will we sit idly by while our allies are bullied or attacked. Since this action, I have been informed by our military leaders that the Chinese buildup has begun to turn back towards China. While we continue to monitor the situation, I have ordered all military to remain at the severe threat level and be prepared to take whatever action is necessary to counter any threat.

Thank you, and God Bless the United States. In the remaining few minutes, I will take questions," stated the President, pointing to members of the press.

Chapter 14: The Wedding Gift

With his military duty to Country behind him, a small church wedding was planned for Karen's birthday, June 17th. Karen looked glamorous in an antique white sheath wedding gown with a slim profile that closely followed the curves of her body and set off her sparkling baby blue eyes, copper toned tan and shoulder-length hair. Ray dressed reserved and elected to wear his military dress uniform. And for best man, there couldn't be anyone better suited than his best friend, Jack Walsh.

As immediate family and friends entered the church and were escorted to their seats, the wedding was to be underway shortly. The church parking lot was completely filled and no extra parking along the street could be found.

"Hey, Jack? What's going on? Someone said we have run out of parking spaces. Where are all these cars coming from?" asked Ray, catching up to Jack, standing next to the church entrance, and greeting people as they arrived.

"You look great Ray. I took the liberty of inviting a few extra people, but don't ask. And don't worry about the parking. I've taken care of it," replied Jack.

"You have the ring, right?" asked Ray.

"Just relax and let everything take its course," responded Jack, patting Ray on the shoulder and motioning him to take his place at the Alter as the sound of the church organ started. "You're on."

Ray was handsome standing at the altar, showing the air of confidence. And Jack was right beside him, just in case he needed assurance. The room was silent as the organist began the traditional *Wedding March* and Karen and her mother, Trudy, proceeded down the aisle. Every head turned. The only sounds heard were the sounds of joy being reflected from the women tearing up. The wedding was preceded by church services, then followed by the wedding vows. Side by side, Ray and Karen said their vows. Then the time came for the exchanging of the rings.

"Jack, do you have the ring?" asked Ray in a low voice. Jack was silent, gazing towards the back of the Church for several seconds. "I think so," he responded, searching through his pants and coat pockets.

The seconds ticked by as Jack appeared to look for the ring, while continuing to focus his attention towards the rear of the Church.

"Jack, where's the ring?" asked Ray again.

"I don't .." was the start of Jack's response, but was cut short by a commotion at the back of the Church. Everyone turned in disgust and stared to see what was going on. Then, from behind the standing onlookers, emerged the President of the United States, and First Lady, flanked by secret service.

"Sorry I'm late, but it's a media frenzy out front," said the President in a low tone of voice, hurrying down the aisle.

"Don't worry, I've got the ring" replied Jack, patting Ray on the back as the President made his way up to stand beside him.

"I apologize for the disruption, please continue," stated the President, looking towards the minister and then at Karen, giving her a smile and a wink. Ray asked Jack again for the ring. Jack removed the ring from his coat pocket, handed the ring to the President, who in turn handed it to Ray. Ray held Karen's hand and placed the ring firmly on her finger.

With the vows completed, Ray and Karen kissed before heading out of the Church to be showered with rose pedals and rice, along with the continued photos and videos from the President's entourage of news media paparazzi. Ray and Karen made it through the media blitz before getting into the Ford pickup to head home, and get ready for the wedding reception.

"Hold up a second Ray," shouted Frank, as he made his way to the truck. "I just talked to Maggie. She said you can take Karen to pick up your wedding gift whenever you're ready. It's only a fifteen minute drive each way, and you will be back in plenty of time for the party," said Frank, in a low voice, leaning over the truck door.

"Thanks dad. We'll go home and change before we drive up," stated Ray.

"What's that all about?" asked Karen. "What wedding present?"

After a quick change and trying to avoid Karen's questioning, they headed up to Carl and Maggie's farm, north of Danbury.

"Where are we going?" questioned Karen, snuggling against him and prodding him for information.

"You'll just have to be patient," responded Ray. "We'll be there soon."

Ray pulled into the long driveway flanked by white rail fences on each side leading to the main house and several stables. "You bought a horse?" exclaimed Karen.

Maggie was washing down their antique Ford pickup in the driveway when they pulled in. "Just giving her a good wash," shouted Maggie, as Ray and Karen exited from the car

"A Ford pickup? You got another pickup?" was all Karen could get out.

"Carl was supposed to wash this old truck, but if I didn't do it, he would let it sit there until it rained. Let me look at you. Why you're as handsome as ever," exclaimed Maggie, putting down the hose and giving Ray a hug. Then Maggie turned to Karen, and gave her a hug and kiss on the cheek.

"Congratulations. The wedding was just beautiful. Come on, there over in the stable," stated Maggie, in an excited voice, as she turned and motioned Ray and Karen to follow her into the stable.

Maggie peered through the top rungs of the stall door. "Ok, it looks like we're clear," she said as she pushed the door open to expose nine chocolate Labrador puppies. "Quick, grab that one before he gets away. They're fast little guys," Maggie said, laughing, as she tried to contain the rest of the litter.

"Hey girlfriend," Ray said, in a soft voice, kneeling down and giving Cody a hug and kiss. "Are these puppies all yours?"

"Wow, they're so small and so adorable," responded Karen, gazing at them and smiling.

"Pick anyone you like. It's our gift for your wedding," stated Maggie.

"How about that one over there? He has a deep, dark chocolate color," stated Ray, pointing at one of the more aggressive males.

"You've always had an eye for quality," responded Maggie. "He's the pick of the litter."

"Oh no, that one over there!" exclaimed Karen, pointing to a plump female laying in the corner by herself. "That's the one I want," she said excitedly, picking the puppy up. Karen held the puppy close, as it licked her face up one side and down the other.

"Well, congratulations! It looks like you're now parents," laughed Maggie, counting the puppies to make sure they were all there before shutting the stall door.

"Thanks Maggie. Thank you honey," Karen said in a soft voice, holding Ray around the waist and giving him a hug. "This is the best gift I've ever had. And a special thanks to you too, Cody," she said in a comforting voice, kneeling down and hugging Cody.

"We know exactly what we're going to name her," Karen said, holding the puppy close to her as she climbed into the front seat. "We're going to name her *Heidi-Ho*."

"Well, the two of you and Hieid-Ho better get on out of here if you're going to make it to your wedding party!" exclaimed Maggie in an energetic voice, as Ray walked around the truck to get in.

"You and Carl are coming to the party, aren't you?" asked Ray.

"Don't worry about us, we'll be there as soon as Carl gets out here. Meanwhile, you better get home and change for your reception," responded Maggie, closing the truck door.

"We'll see you there," stated Karen, excitedly, holding Heidi-Ho close. Ray turned the ignition key to start the truck. Errrrrr. Errrrrrrr.

"Now what? Why me?" exclaimed Ray in a frustrated voice as he hit his head against the steering wheel.

"Honey, I think you left your lights on and ran your battery down," said Karen, smiling.

"You pop the hood and I'll get the jumper cables," responded Maggie, yelling back as she headed towards the garage, laughing.

The End